IF HITLER COMES

Our authorised representative in the EU for product safety is
Easy Access System Europe, Mustamäe tee 50, 10621 Tallinn, Estonia
gpsr.requests@easproject.com

IF HITLER COMES
A Cautionary Tale

By

DOUGLAS BROWN

and

CHRISTOPHER SERPELL

faber and faber

First published in August 1940
under the title of 'Loss of Eden'

This edition first published in 2009
by Faber and Faber Ltd
Bloomsbury House, 74–77 Great Russell Street
London WC1B 3DA

Printed by Books on Demand GmbH, Norderstedt

All rights reserved
© Douglas Brown and Christopher Serpell, 1940, 1941

The right of Douglas Brown and Christopher Serpell to be identified as authors of this
work has been asserted in accordance with Section 77 of the
Copyright, Designs and Patents Act 1988

This book is sold subject to the condition that it shall not, by way of
trade or otherwise, be lent, resold, hired out or otherwise circulated
without the publisher's prior consent in any form of binding or cover other than
that in which it is published and without a similar condition including this
condition being imposed on the subsequent purchaser

A CIP record for this book is available from the British Library

ISBN 978–0–571–25409–5

AUTHORS' NOTE

AMONG the characters in this story are some very prominent
personages, who are given the names they bear in real life;
but all those which are not thus identified are imaginary, and
have no relation to any living individual.

FOREWORD AND DEDICATION

THE New Zealander who is supposed to write this book is as remote as that other foreshadowed by Macaulay. No-one believes he would ever have the opportunity of telling this sad tale of Britain's decline and fall. But, in fighting this war, it is as well to have in our mind's eye a picture of what would happen to us if the Germans won, either through persuading us to accept a dishonourable peace or (what is equally unlikely) through gaining the victory in the field.

This is no fanciful picture. It is painted from life, with England as the background instead of Bohemia or Poland or any other country now under the Nazi heel. It is not intended to cause despondency or alarm, but to confirm and justify that resolution with which we are now fighting.

If such a tale is to have a dedication it can only be

to

THOSE WHO WILL NOT LET THIS HAPPEN

CONTENTS

	EXTRACT FROM THE RECORDS	*page* 9
	PROLOGUE	11
1.	FORCED FRIENDSHIP	16
2.	"BLOOD IN BRITAIN"	29
3.	FACILIS DESCENSUS . . .	39
4.	STRANGE NUPTIALS	52
5.	A LIGHT THAT FAILED	60
6.	FIXTURE AT LORD'S	76
7.	TERROR	85
8.	UNDER THE YOKE	100
9.	VALHALLA IN SYDENHAM	109
10.	OUTWARD BOUND	124
	EPILOGUE	136

EXTRACT FROM THE RECORDS
of the New Zealand Society of Pre-Cataclysmic Research

EDITED BY PROFESSOR APA-KE-MAUI

THE *document which I have the privilege of submitting to members of the Society in this volume of the Records was recently discovered during excavations on the site of the former City of Wellington, which was overwhelmed by the volcanic disturbances occurring in the Antipodes at about the time when the greater cataclysm struck the Continent of Europe. The find, which was made by my assistant, Mr. Rowatorua, is important as being the longest and most complete printed document yet discovered on this site. It was unearthed at the bottom of a deposit of charred and confused literary fragments—probably the remains of a public library—which will require much careful deciphering and editing before they can be made available to members of the Society. This document, however, appears to lack only the first twenty-one pages, and is otherwise in so perfect a condition that it was felt by the Committee that it should be published at the earliest possible opportunity.*

As an archaeologist and not an historian, I am not entitled to offer much comment on the contents, and an authoritative volume of historical notes on the text will shortly be published by my friend and colleague, Dr. Omawei, of Auckland University. As the reader will see for himself, the document takes the form of a quasi-historical record of events occurring towards the end of the second world war of the Twentieth Century as they were witnessed by the writer. The standard of material culture depicted agrees with all the discoveries made by archaeologists investigating that period, and from this point of view the work should be of valuable assistance to us in enlarging and making more detailed our picture of the civilization of the period.

Whether the work can be trusted as an accurate record of events is another matter. The writer, one Charles Fenton, about whom nothing is known except those details with which he himself provides us, was a "correspondent"—in other words a contributor living abroad—of the Wellington Courier, *one of the daily news-sheets which used to be published at a low price during his epoch; and it is known from numerous contemporary references that "journalists", as such men were called, were notorious for the sensational and inaccurate reports which they circulated. Fenton's account of events, although not apparently written in a spirit of levity, does not entirely agree with the theory of world development at that time as it has been formed by modern historians, and it has accordingly been suggested that the document should be regarded as a work of fiction. It is pointed out, for instance, that he does not record the exact year in which the events he describes took place. On the other hand it is clear from in- ternal evidence that they can be ascribed to the fifth decade of the Twentieth Century, and there are several references to incidents and developments which are known to have occurred during the German bid for hegemony. My personal view is that the work, although commonplace in style and to some extent distorted in outlook, may prove of value to both historians and sociologists.*

In conclusion I may say that it had been hoped to illustrate the text with photographs of recent discoveries made by archaeologists both here and in Europe. This unfortunately has proved to be impossible, but I cannot do better than to refer members to the admirable volume of drawings recently published by Mr. Rota-iki-pa-wei, after his return from the Society's expedition to the site of the ancient city of London. His sketch of the ruins of St. Paul's Cathedral drawn from a precarious perch on a broken arch of London Bridge, and accompanied by an imaginative reconstruction of the same scene during the period of its prosperity, is a fine example of how even the dry bones of antiquity can be revived by the artist's visionary eye.

PROLOGUE

. . . speech at Hamburg in January was the most effective of his career. It made him master of half the world. He did not follow it up with pamphlet raids but let it sink in of itself, helped by some feckless pronouncements by British Cabinet Ministers and journalists. I happened to listen in to it at home (quite accidentally, because no-one at that time thought German speeches of much significance), and at once I began to be anxious. I cabled, of course, that the British public would know how to respond to this familiar blend of threats and promises. I wish I had not been lying.

Some of the newspapers, prompted by the Press Department of the Foreign Office, were foolish enough to answer the speech in detail. It was then that one overheard some ominous comments in the street. Ideas had certainly been put into people's heads. "I wonder if he really meant what he said about wanting to treat the Czechs and Poles decently if we only let him alone? Certainly the Scandinavians don't seem too badly off." . . . "It is quite true; the French Government did let us down." . . . "Between you and me there is something in what he says about letting bygones be bygones, and calling it quits." . . . "Well, there must be room in the world for both countries, and if it was anyone else but Hitler" . . . "He didn't even ask for colonies." . . . "Mind you, Russia is the real enemy." . . . "It's a senseless war, really. I can't bear to think of those poor starving children in Germany."

Thus it began—with half-serious comments in pubs and buses, inspired I believe not mainly by real cowardice or lack of resolution, but by a queer blend of simple humanity and sheer weariness of discomfort and anxiety. In both Britain and Germany trade was being ruined; in both Britain and Germany home life was being destroyed, and the women and children were suffering. Blood all the time was being uselessly spilled. And now Hitler, in apparently chastened mood, offered an end to all this. It was such a simple solution—just the "Cease Fire", the *status quo nunc.*

The Government, the Services, the trade unions—all that complex of ruling elements which had taken charge of the British war effort—heard little of these whispers; and they were too closely engaged in the struggle to entertain these doubts themselves. But there were others who had their ears to the ground, and who welcomed thankfully the first spontaneous rumblings of mass pacifism in Great Britain. Peace to them meant dividends, concessions, cartels; it meant escape from the heavy taxation on profits and all the other restrictions which the war effort had imposed on private enterprise; it foreshadowed a triumphal rise through a post-war slump to a new boom; and possibly a more profitable war later on. Above all, since it implied the abrogation of the German-Russian Pact, it meant the banishment once again of the dread spectre of Bolshevism.

As I say, I must leave it to someone more detached than I to describe the slow evaporation of England's fighting spirit. It was the most despairing task of my career to go on sending encouraging messages to New Zealand, when every day I learnt more about the organized letters to M.P.s, the whispering campaign in the clubs, the commercial pressure brought through neutral countries. I have reason to believe that by the summer a complete plan of an Anglo-German financial set-up was already being keenly discussed in City offices.

When Parliament began to reflect the new movement a fissure rapidly revealed itself. The parties supporting the National Government were rent from top to bottom, and out of the confusion that pathetic idealist, Matthew Evans, emerged as the last Prime Minister of the United Kingdom. "No shameful peace, no selfish war," ran his queer slogan, and it was of course a cry of surrender. Behind him stood that "able man" Sir John Naker, the new Foreign Secretary.

Hitler waited a week, and then, early in September, seized the glittering prize. He issued his brief appeal—for "Anglo-German co-operation in a world that is crying out for peace founded on justice". Oddly enough, I cannot now remember how I felt at this time, or the kind of remarks I made to my wife, to my colleagues, to the man who cut my hair. Did we just talk about the weather and the revival of commercial football pools? The lazy blue skies hung over an autumnal and unreal England and it was in a dreamlike frame of mind that I stepped into the plane that was to take me to the signing of the Peace of Nuremberg.

I hardly awoke from my dream during the four days I was in Germany. Our representatives solemnly went through the motions of co-operation with our late enemy to build a better and a happier Europe, and the only real unpleasantness was caused by the presence of the captive French, Czechs, Poles, Scandinavians, Dutch, Flemings, and Walloons, brought to initial the constitutions of their "autonomous" republics.

I was surprised that the Führer refrained from openly

gloating. He remained quite impassive, but ominously self-assured. Ribbentrop—what an escape that man had had!—could not altogether avoid the bearing of one who had finally triumphed against odds, but he observed the decencies. Evans was pale and intense, and somehow dignified. It was only Sir John Naker whom I wanted to kick out on to the Kornmarkt: his smile was so beautifully eloquent of hypocrisy and greed.

During the private discussions I walked about the impressive galleries of the Germanic Museum, reflecting on the extraordinary capacity of this race to create and destroy. But there was not long to wait; Hitler had everything cut and dried. It was not like Munich. There was no sense of drama, because the struggle was over.

I waited for the Nazi Party Rally, the postponed Rally "of Peace", to which the British delegation were invited as guests of honour. I saw poor Evans, looking for all the world like Ramsay MacDonald, wearily watching the hordes goose-step past, and responding now and again with an apologetic Nazi salute.

"Not thus doth Peace return!" This time, it will be remembered, there was no waving from the balcony of Buckingham Palace. The popular reaction was less one of relief than of guilty satisfaction. Here was what we had asked for, and it was for us now to make the most of it.

The necessary moral obtuseness was soon acquired. Had consciences remained tender life would not have been worth living. I remember saying good-bye to a Polish colleague, a man lately fêted as a representative of our noble ally. He was one of many of his race who were "extradited" at the instance of the German-controlled Government in Poland; in fact, Britain had betrayed him. Yet I was quite capable of murmuring something about adapting oneself to the new conditions, and he made a wry smile. It is not easy to adapt oneself to the conditions in a concentration camp. The French who had taken refuge with us quietly disappeared under a thin smokescreen of regretful courtesies.

From our new selfish point of view, things jogged along all right at first. Even my own messages to a shocked Dominion held just enough of enthusiasm for the brave new world in which Germany and Britain claimed a joint leadership. No miracles happened, but people half expected something more disconcerting, and that didn't happen either. After an earthquake it must seem a complete answer to prayer if one's own house is left standing; and here was the political, financial and economic structure of the British Empire still intact. We prodded it a little gingerly; it did not give way. That was enough. Let Hitler settle as he thought best the problems of south-eastern Europe—that was his responsibility. Let France go her own way—our new statecraft had proved we could do without her. And had we not found a room in Hampton Court for the former Polish Ambassador?

Demobilization was our first concern. It was a pity it was not also Hitler's, but then he had become our bulwark against Bolshevism again, and Ribbentrop did not turn a hair. The great wave of unemployment was rather disconcerting, but it was obvious, as the Chancellor of the Exchequer said, that a new prosperity was waiting round the corner, now that Europe was dedicated to eternal peace. Much was to be expected of the comprehensive trade agreement being thrashed out with Germany—the big London hotels were full of the delegates, whom you could tell by their ostentatious Swastika armbands.

It was curious how cynical we tried to become in our defeatism. Yet we talked a good deal about the Navy, and it was arranged to hold a Spithead review in the summer. There were plenty of hidden doubts about the future, but the prevailing mood was nostalgic. Something very precious had passed silently from the, national life.

> *No more to watch at night's eternal shore,*
> *With England's chivalry at dawn to ride;*
> *No more defeat, faith, victory—Oh! no more*
> *A cause on earth for which we might have died.*

When the real troubles began we bore them stoically. "An inevitable period of friction and readjustment," the Prime Minister called it—and in this he included the I.R.A. bombs, the Communist strikes, the troubles in India, and the extraordinary nuisance value which our latest native brand of Fascists, the Greyshirts, were acquiring. You will not, I am afraid, find a particularly full account of these latest developments in the files of the *Wellington Courier*, or of any other newspaper. No-one wrote about trends, and the troublesome events seemed to happen in a vacuum. Parliament had got itself adjourned, and there was little demand for its recall; editors were told that the quickest way of restoring confidence was to refrain from too much comment. We concentrated on Utopian visions of the future, and on the lighter side of life. "Crisis" was an outmoded word. There were still enough people making handsome profits out of the peace.

On Friday, 10th March, of the fateful year that followed

the peace, my wife Elizabeth and I, with our young child Julia and her nurse, went down to spend a long week-end with friends at Debenford. There was no news about, we said in Fleet Street—in fact, we were always complaining about the absence of news. Labour troubles in the North, the usual depressing cables from Calcutta, some Jews beaten in Whitechapel—none of this was news to a case-hardened England. Now if Hitler would give some indication of his future policy, it would be different. The coming of the new era awaited his word. Even a hint or two that he would like some colonies back would have been a relief. But he was strangely silent, while all that Goebbels could talk about was the influence the Jews had over the policies of the United States.

Yes, it was safe to take a holiday, and seek the first signs of spring in the byways of Suffolk. The world had had a surfeit of high politics, and the chief virtue of the Peace of Nuremberg, as an ex-Prime Minister had said (forgetting that there were still 2,000,000 men under arms in Germany, and that Europe was full of refugees), was that it sent men back to the corners of the earth to which they belonged, there to rediscover the simple and abiding things. What if we had sacrificed some of our imperial pretensions, and had become a humbler people? We had purged away dross, and could the better treasure the gold. The swans gliding on the Deben and the ploughman crossing by the evening ferry perhaps knew a secret of happiness denied to those who had gone out and built empires.

It was an incomplete philosophy, and would have appeared so among the harassed Friday-night shoppers in the East End. The great crowds cannot step aside from history; and in our hearts we knew that even the peace of the Suffolk marshes was a prize of war, only to be defended by the same determination that once drove back the marauding Danes.

That night, while the high tide flushed silently into Martlesham Creek, Downing Street received an urgent telephone call from Heir Hitler in Berlin.

Chapter One

FORCED FRIENDSHIP

THE best-remembered blue sky is that from which a bolt has fallen. But I will not stop to describe Debenford, its trees, its flats, its shining estuary, its vicarage, and grand old church. They, with our friends there, and Ashdene Cottage, are symbols which no-one else would wish to bother about. All I will affirm is that when the crisis of Saturday, 11th March, overtook us we were in a place we shall always remember and that we believe to have been one of the pleasantest spots in the world.

It was a matter of looking at the *Daily Express* when I came down to breakfast I had lain overlong in bed listening drowsily to the jubilation of a thrush in one of the tall cedars on the lawn, and had no desire to look at a paper at all. But my host, Gerald Cooke, himself buried in the pages of *The Times*, handed me the *Express* with the remark: "Looks as if your friends in Fleet Street had got the wind up again." With a slight and familiar sinking of the heart I looked at it.

"Another threat of war," the headlines screamed at me. "Germany masses her armies." . . . "Menacing speech by Führer."

The news, when one got down to it, proved to be vague, but none the less alarming. There had been German troop movements towards the north-east, and a Dutch source gave their number as twenty divisions. One knew and mistrusted Dutch sources, but there must be something in it. Hitler had spoken at a gathering of Party leaders at Breslau, reverting abruptly to the intransigent style of his early war speeches. It might be intended only for home consumption, but there were some ugly passages. "The colonial question must be settled here and now. Those who speak of conferences do not realize the temper of the German people. The German people will not plead before a conference table for their rights. They will demand them with a voice of thunder, and no international Jewish combine shall dare to oppose that voice. . . ." Another passage, referring to the armed might of the Reich, "perfected by its recent trial", contained the sentence: "The German Air Force is the strongest weapon that any nation has ever possessed. Others have boasted of their defences, but I say now that if I were to give the word the war-planes of the Reich could take off in their thousands and lay any hostile capital in ruins."

The Times gave the news in more qualified fashion, but did not conceal its gravity. To say that the German troop movements might be only a prelude to the long-promised German demobilization did not exclude the possibility of another less pleasant alternative. Hitler's speech was given in full, and a brief diplomatic commentary deplored its tone, pointing out that a settlement of the questions left outstanding by the war was one of the first objects of the British Government.

"I'm afraid I shall have to run up to Town to look into all this," I said, with a feeble attempt at light-heartedness. "It may prove to be a mare's nest, and in that case I can catch the four-thirty down in time for dinner." Elizabeth looked at me anxiously, and I could feel the concern of our hosts, who, however, took the matter with their customary matter-of-fact calm. It was arranged that my wife should stay on, and that I should telephone as soon as I knew how things were going.

"By the yellow Tiber there was tumult and affright"—in fact all the symptoms of a crisis as pre-war London had displayed them. There was remarkably little news from the Continent, the usual "well-informed sources" having closed down with unanimous rapidity. Officials at the Wilhelmstrasse had declined to comment on the current rumours, merely remarking that, as the Führer's speech had shown, the situation was one of gravity. The Foreign Office in London was equally uninformative: reports from various European centres had been "grossly exaggerated"; the Government were not inclined to view the situation as a crisis: it was true that in view of certain unexpected developments a Cabinet meeting had been called for that afternoon, but this was no more than a normal precaution due to the desire of the Foreign Secretary to acquaint his colleagues with the facts; any tendency to panic was strongly deplored.

If such remarks were intended to have a reassuring effect it was unfortunate that the Home Office should have announced simultaneously that the London A.R.P. organization was to be revived. There was a frenzied remobilization of wardens and ambulances going on all day, and those firms which had discarded their wartime defences of sand-bags and boarded windows looked askance at those which had retained them.

I soon realized that there was to be no return to the country for me that week-end, and rang up Ashdene Cottage. "Is there going to be another war?" Gerald asked, and all I could do was to say that it was best to prepare for the worst.

By six o'clock the Cabinet had risen, but there was no statement forthcoming in spite of the crowds waiting in Downing Street and Whitehall. Privately I learnt that the Government were in continuous touch with Berlin, but no-one was bold enough even to guess at the nature of the negotiations. Fresh reports of troop movements had come in from the Low Countries, and were published in the evening papers, and there was also a story of unidentified aircraft seen flying along the East Coast. Personally I had come to the conclusion that we were to be treated to a display of *Blitzkrieg* at its worst, and had hinted as much in my dispatches to Wellington.

There was an extraordinary atmosphere of helplessness everywhere. If this had not been foreseen by the Government, what could the private man do? Even the attempts to revive A.R.P. were, I was told, half-hearted. I was thankful that Elizabeth and the child were in the country.

At half-past eleven that night, when I was contemplating going to bed in my clothes after a day spent mainly in making fruitless inquiries, some enlightenment was vouchsafed. An urgent message was circulated from the Foreign Office requesting the representatives of all the newspapers to be present in the Locarno Room at nine o'clock the following morning, as an important statement was to be made. Inquiries into its nature were useless, and the infuriated editors of Sunday newspapers had to go to press without satisfaction. They could only record the official announcement broadcast with the late News that His Majesty's Government had been engaged in important and delicate negotiations with the German Government and that it was expected that these would shortly be brought to a successful conclusion. Dubious, but relieved of its immediate fears, the nation went to bed.

The next morning I took my place in a congregation of my colleagues seated rather incongruously on gilt chairs arranged in rows at one end of that august meeting place. Some of us were yawning and bleary-eyed after our labours overnight. Officials, among whom I recognized Billings of the F.O., were gathered at the far end of the great table. Then the door opened, and in walked none other than Ribbentrop himself, bulky in a great fur-collared overcoat, followed by the Prime Minister and Sir John Naker.

There was a mutter from, someone behind me—someone possessing the omniscience of the true reporter which I was never able to achieve: "Flew over in a special plane this morning; arrived at seven-thirty." To me the appearance of the German Foreign Minister was a complete shock, and so it was to many others. I was expecting a temporizing statement, even the announcement of an immediate conference, but the presence of Ribbentrop must mean that everything was settled. There was tense expectation in the air.

The statesmen had taken their seats at the head of the conference table. They were surrounded by officials, some standing on either side of the central group, others hovering in the background. Dr. Evans and Sir John Naker were conferring in low tones over a piece of paper. Ribbentrop sat staring superciliously down the room, apparently bored with the whole proceedings.

Then there was a brief stir as the Prime Minister rose to his feet and looked down the room towards us. A shaft of sunlight from the long windows touched his grey curly hair. We leant forward to catch his cultured, diffident voice—perhaps this time a little more diffident than usual.

"I have invited you here to-day, gentlemen," he said, "as witnesses of an historic act of peace. I am well aware of the rumours which during the past twenty-four hours have been reaching this country from various unauthorized sources—rumours of yet another war, rumours of menaces directed against this country by a Great Power—a crystallization, in fact, of all the irresponsible talk that has been flying about since this country signed a peace with Germany last autumn.

"To-day I am privileged to dispel not only these rumours but something of much greater moment—all fear of war in our time. I am about to put my initials to an instrument which will bind Great Britain and the German Reich in a union closer than has ever before been achieved by two Great Powers, a union which will effectively remove . . ."

Here the precise words, with their sing-song intonation, were drowned in a growing roar which shook the tall sash windows. We turned involuntarily to look, and glimpsed phalanx after phalanx of broad-winged bombers sweeping low across the narrow segment of sky which was visible from our seats. The noise lasted for an intolerable minute, while Evans stood irresolute, fingering a sheet of blotting paper. Then as the roar swept on in a diminuendo over London, Sir John Naker leant forward. "I am advised by the German Foreign Minister", he said in an expressionless voice, "to say that the German Air Force has chosen to celebrate to-day's proceedings with a goodwill flight over London and the other larger cities of the British Isles."

The Prime Minister bowed his acknowledgement and in

a rather shaken manner scrambled to his conclusion. "I am, in fact," he said, "about to initial a Treaty of Friendship and Mutual Assistance with the German Reich, thus confirming the Peace of Nuremberg on a just and reasonable basis put forward by Herr Hitler with the thorough agreement of His Majesty's Government. I believe it will be in accordance with public feeling in both countries."

He stopped, looked towards us almost as if expecting comment, and sat down. A few seconds later he had initialled the document.

After a pause, Sir John Naker came down towards us with the genial Rotarian countenance which he reserved for the Press. "Now, boys," he chuckled, wagging his finger at us like an indulgent schoolmaster, "no questions! no questions! Billings there will let you have a copy of the instrument. Yes, I know it's been sudden, but you'll find it's all for the best. Glad to see you all here so early in the day. Good morning, all." He turned his broad back on us and made his way, with the others, to the door.

We stared at our copies, finding it difficult this time to disentangle the diplomatic verbiage. It was, indeed, a military alliance, by which Germany guaranteed Great Britain, India, the Dominions, and the Colonies, and we the Greater Reich with all its attendant "autonomous protectorates". Each country "recognized as part of its own vital interest the integrity and orderly government of the other". There were to be staff talks, and an exchange of military and naval information. Naval bases in the Mediterranean and elsewhere were to be shared and jointly administered. An elaborate system of trade preferences was to be set up, foreshadowing, it seemed, a customs union. The Mandated Territories, naturally, were to be handed back; but in any case there was to be an "open door" all round, British capital being as free to develop Galicia as German traders to establish themselves on the Gold Coast. There was a lot about "cultural exchanges", and—most ominous of all—a Press pact, by which neither Government would permit its newspapers to attack the other country's political institutions. Lastly, there was something about eternal peace.

Exclamations expressive of varying degrees of surprise, excitement, and dismay accompanied the departing diplomats, and then we all began to shout and gesticulate at once. I can remember feeling rather helpless, with a dim idea that, since the ineluctable processes of history had produced this inevitable document, one could only wait to see what would happen next.

But a journalist must get his story. A thousand questions were waiting to be asked; and there was a rush to consult Billings or some other official of the Press Department. But Billings looked as bewildered as the rest of us. He said there was nothing to add. The treaty spoke for itself, and in any case the Prime Minister would be broadcasting during the evening.

The American who shared my taxi back to Fleet Street was voluble and incoherent. Like me, he must send a message at once, and he was equally at a loss for "a line". He muttered conflicting *clichés*, varying from "Hitler's Paper Triumph" to "The Beginning of the End".

"Who can tell what it means?" he asked despairingly. "A people like this cannot be robbed of their birthright by a hole-and-corner rendezvous at nine on a Sunday morning.

"I am beginning to think it amounts to very little, really," he went on, as the cab cut the corner of Trafalgar Square. "The return of the colonies is the only concrete clause in it; and that was expected. The rest just flatters Hitler's vanity—lets him link arms with a respectable old aggressor like your British Empire. You have got to live side by side in your respective spheres, and there is no harm in drawing up a nice, neighbourly contract in black and white."

He laughed, probably because he knew he was talking nonsense.

The bells of the few Wren churches in the City which had survived the second "Great Fire" were keeping up tradition by summoning to prayer the inhabitants of an unslept-in part of London. The few people in the streets were walking westwards, feeling that the rumours of Saturday night might find some visual expression in the neighbourhood of Downing Street. The special editions were not yet on the streets. A London Sunday morning was still nearly its old, blank self.

Our taximan, however, had heard something of what had happened, and displayed a mild interest in it. When he was being paid he remarked: "So they've been signing another treaty down in Whitehall, have they, gentlemen? Well, after that Nuremberg business, I suppose they might as well make a proper job of it."

What, I wondered, was Hitler's notion of a proper job? After I had sent my first startling cablegram I sat back for a moment, and my eye lighted on an old wartime copy of an illustrated paper. On the cover was a portrait of the Führer, his little eyes glowing with an inexhaustible fanaticism; and inside were some rather unpleasant pictures, smuggled out of Prague.

The tide of excitement soon began to rise, and by dusk the streets and clubs were full. On the whole, to my surprise, it was a pleasurable excitement, and the impression began to gain ground that the Government had cleverly averted another tiresome crisis in cutting the Gordian knot and frankly acknowledging the interdependence of the two greatest Powers in the world. Leader writers were busy describing this "great new experiment in international relations", and one of them was tactless enough (but positively on this occasion only) to write of "new opportunities for the civilizing influence of Great Britain".

Cabinet Ministers contributed nobly to the atmosphere of anti-crisis. Ribbentrop, wise man, had flown back early to Berlin, upon which they felt capable of assuming an attitude of dignified and assured insouciance. They lit complacent cigarettes on the steps of Number Ten, and the Prime Minister, within earshot of a gossip writer, remarked to the Chancellor of the Exchequer that he had decided to make a start with pruning his roses. Sir John Naker threw some crumbs to the pelicans in St. James's Park, dined informally at a popular restaurant, and then went to see the film version of *Merrie England*. All interviews were refused; and not even the Dominions High Commissioners were seen. "The policy of His Majesty's Government," it was officially explained, "of which the agreement with Germany forms a part, can be elaborated only in Parliament, but the Prime Minister will broadcast a statement to the nation at eight o'clock to-night."

The broadcast stands on record as one of history's most celebrated manifestations of unconscious hypocrisy. Everyone wanted to believe it, so it passed. But as soon as that tired but pathetically hopeful voice died on the ether England began talking again, and went on talking far into the night. All had their hopes—the privileged that they would keep their privileges in a world that had become far too restive, the workers that they would catch up with the cost of living, the unemployed that they would find jobs again. Perhaps in a stable balanced Europe all wishes would be fulfilled.

The Greyshirts also had their hopes. They marched down the Mile End Road, and beat up quite a number of Jews before order could be restored by the police.

I was up early next day to read the papers. The Government had a good Press, in the sense that no-one suggested that they might have taken a different course. Each journal in its own way put the best face it could on what had happened. There was nothing anywhere that was constructive, that indicated or commended a policy for the future.

The news columns were more revealing. Dispatches from Germany showed that the crowds in Berlin, in marked contrast to those in London, had spent a Sunday of triumphant rejoicing, culminating with a speech from the Führer in the Sport Palace. That speech was gone over in London with a toothcomb, but, though it contained many expressions of goodwill towards the British Empire, there was no clear indication of what he hoped to do with it in the future. The best indication was perhaps provided by the news that, while he was yet speaking (and anticipating somewhat the terms of the treaty), an unspecified number of troops had set sail from Hamburg, under convoy, to take possession of the former German colonies in Africa.

The interpretative message that I put together that morning was necessarily ill informed, but not more so than anyone else's, and I felt that in a discreet way I had warned my startled readers to expect the worst. Usual sources of information had now completely broken down, and the busy London scene through which I walked to the cable office had suddenly become as remote as that of a strange city. Yet the red buses and the taxis were the same, like the people hurrying up familiar office stairs. It was as though some firm to which one had devoted one's working life had quietly gone bankrupt, but was still being carried on as a going concern by a shadowy Official Receiver.

However, it was not long before I came up against the first signs of inner change. As I was about to hand in my painstaking cablegram the clerk, polite and friendly, said: "Ah, Mr. Fenton, we have a nice little office fixed up for Mr. Johnson already. Smart work, eh? Perhaps you will step along."

In a moment I was standing before a nervous young man who, seated at a trestle table, looked as surprised to be there as I was to find him. The clerk announced me, and withdrew.

"Well, Mr. Fenton," said this unexpected apparition, "I'm from the Foreign Office. It is a matter of glancing at outgoing cables, under the terms of the Treaty. No abuse of the other country's institutions, and so on. A pure formality, of course," he added hastily.

"What is this—a censorship?" I said, amazed.

"Well, no, it's not that," he replied. "It's just that the F.O. thinks it would help the Press in this matter if there is someone at hand who can initial messages before they are sent."

"But why pick on me?" I asked.

"Oh, but this applies to everybody, of course," he said. "I'm here to cover the Eastern Union cablegrams, but there's someone in every newspaper office in London and at all the agencies." He held out his hand for my typescript.

"Well, this beats me," I said. "However, I don't think I'll trouble you. I am prepared to take full responsibility for what I have written."

Then it all came out. Mr. Johnson coughed apologetically, and said: "As a matter of fact, I doubt if the cable company will dispatch the message if I haven't initialled it. Those seem to be the instructions."

So, in this little bare room, standing before a callow youth who was more of a straw than I was on the tide of change that was sweeping over England, I realized that we could no longer take for granted the Freedom of the Press. The young man picked up a blue pencil and poised it helplessly over the flimsy paper. He fumbled a little, initialled each page, and handed the wad back. "This looks all right," he said weakly.

I thanked him, and walked out unhappily. Poor Mr. Johnson, little as he looked the part, was a portent, and a very unpleasant one.

"A tiresome business, this," suggested the clerk, when I gave in the initialled sheets, "but we shall get used to it."

I hurried back to the office, anxious to consult my colleagues upon this new development. On the way I had a bright idea. I called in at the Post Office, and dispatched a private cable to my editor. It ran something like this:

"TODAYS STUFF CANNOT ENTER NATIONAL SINCE ORMONDE RECENTLY ENTERED DERBY FENTON."

At Wellington they tumbled to my elementary code, and that day the staid *Courier* was as effective as any of its rivals in bringing home to New Zealand a sense of great changes. My dignified message was read between the lines by the whole Dominion, for it achieved the distinction, incredible in that time of peace and liberty, of being headed:

> "From Our Own Correspondent,
> LONDON, March 13.
>
> (Censored)"

As a matter of fact, Mr. Johnson, though a portent, was but a temporary one. The Foreign Secretary called the important editors together. With them went my Australian colleague, Dorman, to represent the Dominion journalists, to whom he afterwards reported what had happened. He said that the tiny bubble of optimism that the Government had succeeded in blowing the day before had already burst. Naker had been unable to conceal his anxiety. He had spoken of "Herr Hitler's somewhat natural impatience" and "the necessity of showing the utmost goodwill at the outset", and had declared that "the success of this great experiment" depended altogether upon the discretion of the Press. But the outcry against a Foreign Office censorship had been too much for him, and he had agreed to the withdrawal of Mr. Johnson and his colleagues.

In the afternoon Parliament met. This simple fact was of great comfort to the people. The pre-Hitler machinery of State in the United Kingdom was vast and complicated, with feudal trappings, but the sovereign power ultimately rested with the sober and simple entity known as the House of Commons, and the House of Commons, as was often proudly and ungrammatically declared, "is us". To the average Englishman the authority of Parliament was unchallenged and unchallengeable; subconsciously, he probably believed that its mere assembling would set a term to any unfortunate nonsense that Naker, say, might have been up to.

To be riding in a bus along Whitehall, past the Cenotaph, and to be bound for yet another important debate in the cramped Press gallery of that tawdry, stuffy, and majestic Chamber had a steadying effect upon my nerves. Big Ben struck two, in the tones that meant "heart of Empire" to half the world. A good crowd had gathered, and there was some excitement in Parliament Square. It was caused by one of those tiresome Greyshirt processions, which the police were dispersing. Demonstrations of any kind, it will be remembered, were forbidden within half a mile of the High Court of Parliament.

Among my papers is Hansard for the Thirteenth of March. I have often glanced through it since the day I bought it, and it has assumed in my mind the proportions of a classic tragedy.

"The House met at a quarter before Three of the clock, Mr. Speaker in the Chair." The formula calls to mind that dignified little procession, perhaps the most moving of all the State ceremonial of England, when, preceded by the Serjeant-at-Arms with his mace, the bewigged Speaker walked through the lobbies and the House to his chair. Everyone would bow, and it was an expression, not so much of patriotism, as with cheers for the King, but of an even deeper loyalty to the ancient liberties of which Parliament was the age-long guardian.

How much had not been accomplished in this mock-Gothic Chamber in the course of a century, by the last Parliaments in the long line that went back centuries more! One thought of the wise social legislation brought to fruition, the scandals exposed and ended, the voices of successive statesmen summoning the nation to its constructive tasks. Thus had British democracy and empire been slowly and delicately integrated, through storm and calm, until to-day, it had come to provide the framework of millions of happy and useful lives.

And now this great institution, palladium of English liberties, was still in being, its meeting-place overflowing with the full complement of duly elected members. Everyone, I was told, was there for prayers; and very moving it must have been. Even the Cabinet were in their places, Naker and the rest; but surely those of them (I exclude Evans) who knew what they had done or assented to must have felt like Judas in the Upper Room.

I never mastered British Parliamentary procedure, and cannot explain how it came about that a meeting summoned during the Easter recess to deal with an emergency and to ratify a treaty should begin with a string of questions to Ministers about pensions and municipal finance in West Ham. But I have the clearest recollection of the famous incident that came in the middle of these proceedings, and added to the feeling of tension in the debate that followed.

There was suddenly a great commotion in the Distinguished Strangers' Gallery. It was already stiff with diplomats, but here came the German Ambassador, followed by a suite of seven or eight attachés and brown-shirted secretaries such as had never before been seen in these surroundings. The Dutch and Flemish Ministers, with some others, hastened to make room for them, but they did not at once sit down. Instead, standing to attention and raising their right hands towards the Chair, they interrupted the quavering voice of the Minister of Health with the raucous, staccato cry, like blasphemy in church, "Heil Hitler!"

The Speaker made no sign, but, while the House kept shocked and humiliated silence, a bold member of the Labour Opposition jumped to his feet, and cried: "On a point of order, sir. Will not the officers of the House, in accordance with practice, see that the strangers responsible for this unseemly interruption are summarily ejected?"

The Germans had clattered down into their seats, like a

Roman emperor and his familiars at the circus. There was a pause; the Labour man remained on his feet, while a faint sound of "Hear, hear" came from the benches around him. The Treasury Bench tried to look as though nothing remarkable was happening.

At last the Speaker found his voice. It shook as he took the only dignified course, picking up the thread that had been rudely, perhaps permanently, broken. "The Right Honourable the Minister of Health," he said, looking straight in front of him; and the thin voice that had been interrupted resumed its part in the orderly proceedings of the Mother of Parliaments.

At last the Foreign Secretary rose to open for the Government in the big debate. He had quite regained his self-possession; one could see that he knew exactly what he was going to say, that he was prepared to answer certain objections and determined to ignore others, and that by the sheer force of his personality he intended to keep the debate on the plane of slightly cynical, but genial, common sense.

His brisk, cheerful tones dispelled some of the gloom of the "Heil Hitler!" incident. He was, in fact, brilliantly persuasive. For all his tortuousness he had always been a good Commons man, and he wooed the House like a rather too practised lover. There at least he was sure of himself, however delicately he might still have to tread before the representatives of the Wilhelmstrasse.

There is no need to repeat his arguments. They look false enough now, but most people welcomed them gladly enough at the time, as holding out the one chance of a prosperous and not undignified future for Great Britain. The House listened to them hopefully, but in silence.

He came at length to the circumstances of the last fatal week-end.

"As time went on", he said, "it became increasingly clear to His Majesty's Government and to the Government of the German Reich that the new situation should be clarified and crystallized, for all the world to see, in a treaty of friendship and mutual assistance. This instrument, freely negotiated, is that which the House——"

It was here that the first interruption occurred. There were cries of "Question", and Churchill was first on his feet to ask with calm deliberation whether His Majesty's Government, in these "free negotiations", had been uninfluenced by the fact that Germany on the previous Thursday had begun the transport of twenty divisions from the interior to the north-east coast.

"And by Hitler's threat on Friday night to bomb London to bits," added a bold member of the Labour Opposition, guessing at the truth.

Almost the whole House was now on its feet, the Opposition back-benchers emboldened at last to make a demonstration, screaming "Traitors!" at the Government, and the Government members calling "Mischiefmakers!" in reply. The Speaker made no attempt to quell the tumult, and Naker remained seated until it had died down. Then (says my Hansard):

"Honourable members opposite", he said (with a deprecating gesture of his hands), "are inclined to ignore the processes of history. Their antique jingoism has little meaning to-day. One could not but admire their valour (were it ever put to the test), but we on this side of the House prefer a higher patriotism. To us the British Empire is no mere temporary phenomenon, consistent with but one phase of historical development. We do not seek to preserve it by vainly trying to keep the rest of the world unchanged; we seek to develop it by meeting changing conditions in a spirit of realism and co-operation."

So he went on, and no interruptions could break his apparent complacency. He became very plain and matter-of-fact, almost casual, and in a bare twenty minutes he had finished the speech in which, as British Foreign Secretary, he virtually handed his proud country to the mercy of the enemy. But when he sat down there was sweat on his forehead.

Some of the speeches that followed, on the Opposition side, were almost worthy of this great and tragic occasion. One notable Tory Parliamentarian evoked the great leaders of past times, who would have wept had they seen the extremity to which modern leadership had brought the nation. Labour leaders spoke of painfully won social reforms, and asked who would be their guardian now. All pleaded that the House might, at the last moment, take a mighty risk to redress a great error; all, at the same time, clearly knew they were making valedictory speeches.

On the Government side there was gallant wishful thinking. Backbenchers exhibited a renewed faith in Nazi promises, and the Lord Privy Seal almost made it appear that Great Britain, out of sheer altruism, had condescended to help Germany in her European problems. "Naught", he said, with sublime inappropriateness, "shall make us rue."

Chamberlain's unforgettable speech will find its way (if civilization survives) in the school history books. "Peace was my life's ambition, but not this peace." His voice trembled when he said that it was his faith in his country's courage and integrity that had enabled him to make the great experiment of Munich. Could it be that faith was unjustified?

Evans rose to wind up the debate. One was aware of the strange similarity between the two men. They had many ideals in common, and were equals in sensibility, but Evans had no strength of character.

The House held its breath. Who knows but that in that brief moment there lay the chance that a great leader might have seized, to rescue England, if not from destruction, then from shame? Did the House feel that the shades of Pitt, Disraeli, Gladstone were crowding round the last holder of their great office, begging, even commanding him to shrink from the final betrayal? If so, the moment passed, and soon members were settling down to listen to an uninspired recapitulation of all the arguments which, during the last six months, had been brought to defend a policy of surrender. There was a sense of anticlimax as, rather unexpectedly, the Prime Minister sat down; and the question was put. No-one had the heart to challenge a division; the last formalities were rapidly attended to; and, in the midst of an intolerable silence, the Speaker rose and left the Chamber. British democracy, fruit of centuries of struggle on this hallowed spot, had gone by default.

Few of the faithful Commons could trust themselves to speak, either to themselves or to the familiar, courteous attendants, as they struggled into their overcoats and were gone. "Who goes home?" Many, many things, that would not bear thinking of.

Chapter Two

"BLOOD IN BRITAIN"

FATE, you may remember, allowed Sir John Naker three days in which to enjoy the full triumph of his foreign policy. Three spring-like days they were, so that, discarding an overcoat, he could walk jauntily across the Park each morning to the Foreign Office, surveying, through the burgeoning trees, the gallant towers of Westminster, symbols of the mighty State machine that he had set rumbling on the course he had chosen for it. They were honeymoon days, with the diplomatic wires buzzing with congratulatory messages, from Göring, from Ribbentrop, from Hitler himself, while the British Press played up nicely and the Stock Exchange boomed. There was no need for him to listen at Cabinet meetings to the tale of woe of the Minister of Labour; he, Naker, had now provided the international conditions for a trade revival, and it was for the other fellows to take advantage of them. Still less need he bother much with the Egyptian Ambassador who kept anxiously asking for certain assurances, and for a promise of mediation in some incipient dispute; trust him, Naker, not to interfere in anyone else's *Lebensraum*. Soon it would be time to settle some of the details of the brave new world, and Hitler's State visit, expected in May, would be a busy time for him; meanwhile, he felt he could afford to climb with leisurely aplomb into the biggish niche that history, he was sure, had provided for him.

So I read his attitude, but I do not pretend to know what came into his mind when the three days were over and the ground opened before his feet. I do not know whether even then he foresaw the full disaster, or whether the thing that meant so much for the rest of us had little or no significance for him. He was a man without roots, patrician or plebeian, and he could have been betrayed by his cynicism into grave miscalculations.

But none of us, indeed, had realized quite how large a place the monarchy played in British nationhood. When the *Renown* slipped silently out of Plymouth Sound, flying the last Royal Standard ever rightfully to flutter in an English breeze, it took away more than the Crown. It took away our faith in our future and in ourselves. Constitutional propriety allowed only this supreme rebuke from the monarch to his people. There had never been a juster one.

The quiet honeymoon was over. Shorn of our ancient symbol of continuing tradition, we found ourselves face to face with grim reality of the present. We felt uncomfortable when Herr Hitler sent a telegram of congratulation to our makeshift, and probably unconstitutional, Council of Regency, upon their good fortune in "opening a new and glorious chapter in Anglo-German Nordic history". We were afflicted with painful doubts about the legal status of the British Empire, under the Statute of Westminster. We trembled when we came to examine the problems that demanded solution at home.

"Watch the Greyshirts" came as an entirely unnecessary admonition from my editor. Who in England was not now watching them? Within a few days, wherever Englishmen met and talked the same question was asked: "What will the Greyshirts do now?"

Looking back, I am ashamed to think that I had not paid more attention to the rise of Fascism in England. It was an alien, injected poison, but when the right conditions for its growth appeared it began to flourish soon enough.

Our body politic had long before been deliberately inoculated by the adroit pathologists of Nazi expansion. The technique which, after years of careful tending, turned Austria into a hotbed of sedition, which converted the Sudeten Germans from a comparatively passive minority into a raging fever of protest, and which pushed the Trojan horse into Norway, Holland, and Belgium, was from the very outbreak of hostilities directed towards fomenting divisions and dissensions not only between the chief Allies but between parties and bodies of opinion in both nations.

For a time these efforts had no results. Goebbels undoubtedly thought at the beginning that the tolerant atmosphere of a democracy would present an ideal field for his experiments. He forgot that he was attacking a healthy body, which centuries of open political discussion and criticism, and the traditions of a free Press, had immunized against the poison of seditious propaganda. A few pacifists, purblind with the immature ideals of youth, could be found to heckle the public speeches of Ministers and glory in the martyrdom of being expelled by the police. The I.R.A. could be subsidized to distribute a few bombs and so-called Communists could be bribed to foment disorder, but the British public could never be persuaded to adopt the right terrified attitude towards the melodramatic type of agitator. It was only mildly indignant at an added inconvenience to existence. Thus the first German attempts to introduce sedition failed miserably. People were too absorbed in the magnitude of the task undertaken by the nation to pay much attention to those who sought to sow doubts; and where there were just grievances the Constitution still allowed a remedy.

Demobilization brought back into the civilian life thousands upon thousands of young men who had thrown up jobs and prospects to fight for the ideals which had now been betrayed. They came back disillusioned and exasperated. They had experienced all the boredom and misery of war, and all its horrors; some of them had even tasted its triumphs on the field of battle. But their determination and their endurance had suddenly been nullified by the action of "politicians" and they were faced with an intolerable anticlimax. All were convinced that they would have "brought it off" if they had been given a chance. Consequently, from the very beginning, the mood of the average demobilized man, with his weather-beaten old-young face and the green "Nuremberg ribbon" in his button hole, was one of sulkiness and wounded pride. But he was to suffer a worse blow yet. He and nine-tenths of his fellows had been assured that their jobs would be kept for them when they came home. Now they were to find that industry was hard put to it to absorb one-third of their numbers. No-one had taken their jobs: the jobs had simply ceased to exist. Firms which had begun the war by complaining of being short-handed had very soon begun to be thankful for their depleted pay-roll. Now there was no question of rapid expansion. Supplies were still short, and demand was restricted by the thin purse of the average citizen.

I remember talking to one of these men early in January. I met him in a small public house off Fleet Street where both he and I had taken shelter from a heavy downpour soon after opening time. He had just been to see his old firm—he was a paper-maker—and his former manager, who had been, I gathered, kindly though firm, had tried to explain the position to him. The bar was empty except for us two at first, and he had perforce to unburden himself to me.

At first his mood was one of blank bewilderment. Here was he, a man of twenty-eight, with a wartime wife and a mother to support, with his bounty nearly spent, and with the foundation of his existence, his "safe" job, suddenly removed from beneath him. What on earth were they going to do now? His mother had run a small lodging-house for respectable working-class folk before the war, but that had petered out after six months, "what with evacuation and all". Then he had married Renee on leave, and Renee had secured a job in a munitions factory on which she had been able to support herself and his mother. Renee's job had come to an end just before he was "demobbed", and they hadn't minded then, because his civilian job was good enough for them both, and he didn't hold with the wife going out to work. Now they were left without anything.

"There's no kid, anyway," he said slowly. "We were meaning to have one when the war ended . . . but now, well, we'll just have to change our minds."

After a couple of drinks his mood had changed to one of self-pity and an outraged sense of justice. It was no longer what Renee and Mother were going to say that mattered—

it was what his boss had said to him—Joe Richards—when he left to join up.

"He shook me by the hand, and he said:' Richards, there'll be a place for you here when the show's over.' That's what he said. 'The firm will look after you,' he said. That was a promise, wasn't it?"

The story of this parting interview was repeated several times, with mounting indignation. He wouldn't have put up with that perishing cold and that stinking mud and that asterisked sergeant if he hadn't thought that a promise was a promise. Not only the economic but the moral foundations of life had been shattered for Joe Richards by this second interview with his manager. If the boss wasn't going to keep his word, who in this world was?

By this time the bar had filled up, and Joe Richards's audience had swollen. I had murmured my ineffectual sympathy, and it was now being reduplicated profanely and forcibly by a couple of printers, an elderly taxi-driver and a battered old office-cleaner. And as his audience swelled and bought him drinks, so the wrath of Joe Richards mounted, and his eloquence rose to greater heights. I perceived that I was no longer necessary, and unobtrusively retired as yet another round of drinks was bought, this time out of the remnants of the depleted bounty. As I left I had an uneasy premonition that the end of Joe Richards's evening would be a blasphemous encounter with a policeman and a night in the cells.

Joe Richards and his fellows were represented statistically by a catastrophic leap in the already swollen unemployment figure. The harassed Government hurriedly evolved a makeshift programme of public works, intended to absorb some of the labour surplus, but, not unaccountably, men who had once given up skilled jobs to, face the necessary drudgery of military life declined in peacetime to do navvy's work at navvy's rates of pay in road building and land reclamation schemes. They preferred the only alternative—the dole, feeling in their angry misery that they were owed something by their country.

Here at last was a promising culture for infection by the Nazi propagandists, and the virus they chose to start with was inevitable—anti-Semitism. The refugee population of the country had swollen enormously during the years leading up to the war, and, although some misgivings had been felt, the popular sympathy for the victims of the worst type of Nazi brutality had overridden them. Besides, it was then felt that this increase was only a temporary one until Germany was made safe again for non-Aryans. But, by the time the armies were demobilized, many thousands of these hunted people had begun to look on Britain not merely as a refuge in the time of trouble but as a home where they might be safe and free to establish themselves. Had not Britain been waging a war against their persecutors?

Some of the Jews were deeply grateful to their protectors, and did their best to show it. Others, uneducated and inarticulate, merely felt that here at last was the good time coming —the opportunity which mankind owed them in return for their sufferings, a little peace and time to start the business which was their second nature. They had not reached the stage of feeling allegiance to their new country: many of them could not yet speak her language, and in any case were they not themselves children of Israel, a race apart, who through all the centuries of their wanderings had never allowed themselves to be fully absorbed by any other nationality? They were timid and peace-loving; they were incredibly industrious; and they were prolific. It was not for them to realize the problems which their advent would provoke for their new hosts. They were content to obey the laws and asked only the right to work and make a living. Moreover, after their privations, they were ready to begin work for very little. This characteristic appealed, of course, to the employer who was struggling with rising costs; and, although the restrictions on aliens which prevented many of them from being taken into the fighting services applied to some extent to the conditions of employment, a "way round" could often be found, when both employer and would-be employee were willing. Once in employment, their inherent business acumen and their industry stood them in good stead. They were inventive and ambitious, and whenever possible they found vacancies for their brethren.

Thus the Jews became an easy target for all the confused resentment and ill-feeling which was latent in the demobilized unemployed. Anti-Jewish riots broke out more than once in the East End, even before the Treaty of St. James's had been signed. The severity with which they were repressed added fuel to the flames, and the fact that the new Home Secretary, Mr. Bernard Goldsmith, was popularly supposed to be of Jewish descent did not help to keep the peace.

It was about this time that the Greyshirts began to make their appearance under the leadership of the meteoric Patrick Rosse. Long before the war began, when the Government was coping with the ineffectual Fascism of the early 'thirties, there had been legislation against political uniforms, and the "shirt" of various hues had been banned. But the philanthropic War Office, ably seconded by a North Country manufacturer of shoddy, issued each man on demobilization with a complete suit of "mufti", including a grey flannel shirt. When Patrick Rosse began his series of meetings up and down the country it was men in grey shirts who flocked to hear him, and when the League of Britons was formed by the same Patrick Rosse its members wore grey shirts. Who was to forbid them? Who was to deprive the ex-Service man of the gift which his own country had made him?

It is not easy to present a convincing portrait of their leader now. There are so many damning facts, so many equally damning suspicions attached to his history, that it is almost impossible for those who never came into contact with him to imagine the personality of a man who, in spite of his Irish origin and doubtful antecedents, could induce many thousands of Englishmen to follow him over the precipice of their own ruin. There is no doubt that he had been a member of the I.R.A.; his enemies said that he had been one of its leading organizers, but, if that was so, he had abstained from taking any active part in its campaign for some months before the war began. By hook or by crook he then entered the ranks of the British army—according to his enemies as a paid agitator. This at least is doubtful; it may well have been the Irish instinct to join in the biggest fight going. There is no record of his having indulged in any treasonable activity in France; on the contrary he was decorated for gallantry and his promotion was obstructed only by minor incidents of indiscipline which were natural in so obstreperous and reckless a character.

His motives in founding and organizing the League of Britons are equally obscure. Those who regarded Rosse as endowed with a Satanic hatred of England and an equally Satanic ingenuity in accomplishing her ruin believe that the League of Britons was founded with the deliberate intention of building a bridge to the German domination of England, and that it was an I.R.A. conception no less murderous and devastating than a bomb. The complexities of the Celtic mind have always been beyond me, and it is, I suppose, not impossible that a man might give himself up heart and soul to the ruination of a foreign country, if he thought that he could thus free his own. But I find it difficult to believe that anyone with so Machiavellian a turn of mind could inspire his public utterances with the atmosphere of passionate and abandoned sincerity that surrounded the speeches of Patrick Rosse. There is unfortunately no doubt that the League received subsidies from Germany, under the transparent cloak of "gifts from German ex-Service men", and that Rosse was fully aware of this. But I personally do not believe that Rosse fully realized the purpose behind the "gifts". I think he was a man naturally "agin the Government" who became intoxicated with his own popularity and success, and who in his fervour and fury would seize any weapon to attack his adversary.

That is my personal opinion. But I met Rosse and I heard him speak, and I am prepared to admit that anyone who ever fell under the spell of that flaming personality is not a reliable witness. He was the most potent orator I ever heard. It was only a few weeks after the Treaty of St. James's that I went north to attend a big Yorkshire rally of the League of Britons, held in Leeds Town Hall. Unemployment had of course hit the industrial areas hardest, and it was here that the League found its staunchest and most stubborn adherents. Delegations from all over Yorkshire and Lancashire marched into the great hall, each headed with a home-made banner bearing the name of the local branch, and took their places in the rows of red-plush seats under the huge and intolerably bright electric chandeliers. There was nothing theatrical about the gathering—no brass bands and no music from the vast and ornate organ that rose behind the platform and had accompanied so many lusty performances of the *Messiah*. The hall was insufficiently warmed, and I shivered in the Press seats, which were caught by a draught from one of the side-doors. The men about me talked in low tones. There was no smoking: tobacco for this class had become a luxury that was enjoyed only in moments of leisure, and this was not one. Here and there in the crowded hall I could see a woman when I stood up, but it was primarily a male gathering—row on row of serious-faced men, with shabby jackets or overcoats over the inevitable grey shirt.

Then the committee filed on to the platform, and there was a brief stir and a perfunctory clapping from the audience. Still there was nothing to recall earlier outbreaks of Fascism —no roll of drums, no floodlights, and no saluting. Patrick Rosse was easily distinguished from the small group on the platform by his bright red hair and tall stooping figure. He wore a dark suit on which I could see the ribbons of the Military Medal and the Nuremberg decoration. Both he and his companions seemed to the eye of a journalist to be unusually slim and young to be occupying the platform of a public meeting. One was so used to the elderly and well-fleshed committee man.

Lawson, a local journalist, named some of them for me in a whisper. "The scruffy little fellow on the right, who looks like an atheist cobbler, is Morley, the secretary. The chap next to him is a German delegate—think his name's Meyer —he's over on some sort of goodwill mission." (We could not know then that the pale face of Meyer with its fixed smile and staring blue eyes was later to preside over the horrors of the Godalming concentration camp.) "Fellow in the middle is the local chairman—Lewthwaite's his name—and then there's Rosse. Don't know any of the others."

After a few laborious words by the chairman, which included an introduction of "our good friend and late foeman, Herr Meyer" and an acknowledgement of the "handsome donation from our brothers in arms in Germany" which he had brought with him, Rosse rose to speak. I took no notes: I was not there to give a *verbatim* report, only my impressions, and when I later came to write them up I found them incoherent. It was difficult to realize—much less to describe —the way in which that sober, rather stolid meeting was roused to a ferocious and hoarse-voiced mob which went out and did its best to sack the Jewish quarter of Leeds.

It was, to begin with, the strong confident voice, reaching the ears without strain or violence, which disarmed the critical faculties. There was none of the practised lilt of the politician in it; it was not over-educated, and yet the latent brogue was too restrained to become "picturesque" or comic. It was in fact a pleasure just to listen. Then I found myself noticing, with keen appreciation, the extraordinary richness of the man's vocabulary and vivid phrasing. But before long, in spite of all my training, I found myself gripped by his matter. He made the injustices done to ex-Servicemen sound like some huge and legendary crime which must make the world weep. He created bloated giants of oppression, which the feeblest Jack of all longed to rise up and slay. He surrounded us with a labyrinthine web of corruption and inefficiency, and then led us sword in hand to slash our way out. Above all, he depicted the Jew—not the oriental, child-murdering bogy of Nazi doctrine, but the well-to-do smiling alien in our midst —with such venom that even my sanity was clouded with resentment, while half the audience was on its feet baying with fury. Throughout the whole speech he played subtly on the sense of shame which secretly beset so many consciences —a war unwon, a job half-finished, a nation disgraced in the eyes of the world, betrayed by its own half-heartedness and the leaders it had produced. I still remember his peroration, delivered with the voice of a trumpet:

"On your feet. March through the town. Show the Jews and show the world that there is still blood in Britain."

His hearers had leapt up like one man, and, as he ended, streamed shouting and cheering into the city streets.

I sat where I was until my dizzied wits had come to earth. Then I remembered that there was to be an interview with the Press in one of the committee rooms. At this Rosse showed that he was not merely a demagogue. Most of the journalists who were there to question him felt, as I felt, indignant at having been swept off their feet by an oration. They were out to justify themselves as hardened newspaper men, to trip him up and reveal him as a callow politician. They did not succeed. He met their questions with wit and ability, and occasionally abashed them with a quiet sincerity which blunted their would-be cynicism. When he learnt that I was from one of the Dominions his face lit up and he drew me aside to beg that I would convey his message to my own countrymen. Would I ask them, he said, to have patience with the Old Country—to remember that the voice of politicians was not the voice of England? I was to tell them that he and his like were there to restore the lost tradition of Britain, to renew the pride in their heritage which Britons all over the world had once shared between them. The men who had returned sulkily or defiantly to Canada, Australia, and New Zealand would once again be glad that they had sprung to arms. In spite of myself I was moved, not only by his discernment of the feelings which were troubling the hearts of my countrymen, but by the warm, personal friendliness of his manner, and the spontaneity of his words.

Yet even while I talked with him, pandemonium was spreading through the streets as darkness fell over the city. The authorities had been deceived by the quiet and orderly way in which the meeting had begun, and had relaxed their precautions. But what had begun on the Town Hall steps as a tumultuous procession developed within twenty minutes into a riot. It was a Saturday, and the large Jewish population of the city was out enjoying the Sabbath holiday. The sight of the crowded pavements and brightly lit shop windows seemed to enfuriate the Leaguers. One of them levelled his banner-pole like a lance, and with a shout of "Come on, boys, we'll show 'em" dashed it through a window. With the crash of the broken glass rose the ugly, long-drawn sound of women's screaming, and with a roar the fight began. It became the worst kind of street battle. The local citizens fought furiously against the invaders. The Jews among them were not the timid refugees of recent years, but a hardy race born and bred in the industrial slums, and they fought back with the jagged armouries of the race-gangs and the back streets.

The inadequate police forces struggled desperately to regain control, but they were swept aside or trampled underfoot as the battle raged up and down the main shopping thoroughfares. At first the Leaguers, united in a blind enthusiasm, had the upper hand, and drove the crowd before them. Then, as local resentment boiled up and as reinforcements poured out of the public houses and side streets, they in their turn were hurled back. Gradually the main battle broke up into a number of vicious and hard-breathing struggles between small bodies of men, and it was then that the worst casualties occurred. Fortunately by this time the police had collected enough reinforcements to clear the streets, and this they did with repeated truncheon charges and a good deal of very necessary hard-hitting.

By nine that night the battle was over. The pavements were covered with broken glass and wreckage, but the streets were empty except for the police patrols and a few ambulances cruising about to pick up casualties. Leeds Infirmary was full of the wounded, sobbing or shuddering with the sickness that follows mob violence and being tended with grim efficiency by the overworked staff. In the mortuary lay seven broken bodies, two of them in police uniforms, as witnesses that there was "still blood in Britain".

Chapter Three

FACILIS DESCENSUS . . .

THE riot in Leeds marked the beginning of the nightmare period of English history which is not yet ended. Until then the slope into Avernus had been gradual, and the many people who hated the turn events had taken still felt that it was possible to arrest their course and scramble up the insidious incline on to some firm and level ground. But now the abyss opened suddenly at their feet and tune to turn back was not given. Englishmen were plunged into a chaos in which all the things that "don't happen" were dreadfully fulfilled. The friendly half-tones and compromises of ordinary existence seemed suddenly to be resolved into the menacing blacks and blinding whites of improbable drama. Even now, at a distance of both time and space, it is difficult for me to visualize the main actors in that drama as real human beings, and not as portents of perfidy and heroism, oppression and martyrdom.

It is easy, for example, to label Sir John Naker a villain and a traitor; he has been called these names and worse often enough, and yet he was a man who under other circumstances might have lived out an obscure life as a prosperous if none too scrupulous business man. Those of us who met him before he trafficked in his country's liberty thought of him as a not very pleasant character—he was too plausible and genial to carry any honest conviction—but there were other politicians whom we disliked as much, and there were financial magnates whom we suspected of equal dishonesty. We were prepared to believe the gossip-writers when they told us that he was an affectionate parent to his young family, and his expansive after-dinner speeches bore witness that he was an enthusiast for the *genre* novel, with a happy knack of quoting Dickens. But chance, or his own ambition, or the credulity of us, his countrymen, who had grown too prone to substitute mere ability for integrity, placed him in a position in which his ordinary and shabby failings were magnified into an extraordinary betrayal, and Naker the inadequate man was lost for ever in the Naker the arch-traitor. *L'on fait plus souvent des trahisons par faiblesse que par un dessein formé de trahir*.

Two days after I had returned from Leeds I was able to read the German version of the affair, as recounted in the *Völkischer Beobachter*. The British Press, at the urgent request of the authorities, had reduced the incident to a local street affray which had no national significance. There was no attempt to conceal the serious nature of the fighting or the death-roll, which had been swollen when two or three of the casualties succumbed to their injuries, but, deplorable as the disorder had been, it was felt to be too dangerous to lay much emphasis on it. Events were to show how mistaken was this policy. It was no longer the time to hush things up; nerves were too much on edge, and, since the days of the war, official reticence had been regarded as a veil drawn over catastrophe. Now came the German report, compiled by those practised in describing the enormities committed in the unenlightened areas outside the Reich. It appeared that the British police force had been utterly corrupted by Jewish influence and Jewish funds. Together with organized bands of hooligans from "the dance-hall and the gambler's den", this unscrupulous body had made an organized and bloodthirsty assault on a harmless gathering of patriots. There had been unparalleled scenes of cruelty and massacre. There was a heart-rending description of a band of heroes, armed only with "flagsticks", falling in heaps before the "well-aimed volleys" fired by the police. Worst of all, a German had been involved. The war-hero, Meyer, whom the Führer himself had decorated with the Iron Cross, had barely escaped from this holocaust with his life. This was worse than an outrage: it was an insolent defiance of the honour of the Reich. It must be avenged in blood. Meyer, fresh back from England, contributed his "eye-witness account" of these horrors. "German swine" had said one of these English policemen, reeking of slaughter. "Back to your own *verfluchte* country." It is, I believe, a fact that Meyer, suffering from a black eye, had been given a strong police escort as far as Harwich, where he was put on a boat for Germany.

The political repercussions were prompt. On the same day that the account appeared in the German newspapers, the German Ambassador presented himself at No. Ten Downing Street. He was accompanied by a brown-shirted escort similar to that which had attended him in the House of Commons, but this time It was armed with revolvers—"rendered necessary by the civil disorders". He demanded a full-length apology from the British Government for this insult to a German citizen, and substantial compensation for the injuries "he had received at the hands of the police". Furthermore, the German Government insisted that stem reprisals should be taken against the officials involved.

This was the first time that Dr. Evans had come into personal contact with the more downright methods of Nazi diplomacy, and he was worsted badly in the encounter. No details of that interview, which took place at ten o'clock in the morning, are available, but as soon as the German Ambassador had taken his leave the Home Secretary was sent for and requested by the Prime Minister to take exemplary measures of discipline against the constabulary involved in the suppression of the Leeds riot.

Mr. Bernard Goldsmith, the Home Secretary, had been regarded as rather a joke, at least by Fleet Street, up to that time. He was not considered to be particularly competent, and his fussy manner in the House of Commons, together with his sheep-like profile and gold pince-nez, had been favourite material for the cartoonists. His alleged Jewish ancestry had made him the target for the abuse of the Leaguers and their organ the *Free Briton*, which began to appear about this time, but the average man did not take these attacks very seriously. There was nothing of the "sinister Semite" about Mr. Goldsmith—only a catholic enthusiasm for all forms of welfare work and a tendency to take precipitate and rather indiscreet decisions. His reaction to Dr. Evans's suggestion was instant and indignant. He had perfect confidence in the police: their conduct in this unfortunate affair had been admirable. If disciplinary action was to be taken it should be against the disorderly political organization which had provoked the riot. He would listen to no lectures from Dr. Evans on the subject of international tact. Rather than cast any slur on the well-known reputation of the British police force he would tender his resignation. The Prime Minister did his best to soothe him, and the conversation ended without any decision having been made.

Dr. Evans was in a quandary. "People were being very difficult," as he observed pettishly to one of his secretaries, and the situation demanded that worldly wisdom, which, as he had been fond of remarking with mock deprecation from the platform, was abhorrent to his idealistic temperament. Consequently he turned to a source of that commodity which had become habitual to him, and the third visitor to Downing Street that day was Sir John Naker. The result of his advice was startling. The following morning Members of Parliament and the general public read with equal astonishment in their newspapers an open letter from the Prime Minister to Mr. Bernard Goldsmith accepting his resignation, "as tendered orally to me to-day". The letter began in the approved manner, "My dear Bernard"; it paid a cordial tribute to the services which he had performed as Home Secretary, regretted deeply that he had not seen eye to eye with the Government on a matter of policy, and concluded by "Looking forward to the time when we may once more work in harness together". The signature was the signature of Matthew Evans, but there were many who felt that the pen had been the pen of Sir John Naker.

The letter was not accompanied by any explanation or statement from Mr. Goldsmith. That gentleman had of course been rung up by the Press as soon as the letter was circulated, but, although he professed the utmost astonishment at its contents, he refused to comment, reserving the matter, as he said, for the House of Commons.

The House that afternoon threw off for once the dread apathy which had invested it ever since the ratification of the Treaty of London. Every bench was crowded when Mr.

Goldsmith made the statement to which he was entitled. In a voice which trembled with indignation and self-pity he described the conversation in which he had taken part at Downing Street. It was true, he said, that he had conditionally offered his resignation, but had he dreamt that the Prime Minister was contemplating such immediate and underhand action he would have demanded a meeting of the Cabinet. What had he done, he asked, wiping his pince-nez with a shaking hand, to forfeit the confidence of his colleagues? and what had the police of this country done that the word of a single and suspicious alien should be accepted against their official and careful report?

The Prime Minister proceeded to surround the affair with a smoke-cloud of involved eloquence—a screen which concealed the bomb which he exploded with his concluding words. He was pained, he said, by the misplaced emotion which had been engendered by this affair. Mr. Goldsmith's indignation, which had led him to refer in ill-chosen and insulting words to a war veteran of our great ally, had also clouded the conversation at Downing Street, and it was perhaps due to this fact that Mr. Goldsmith had not then made his meaning as clear as it should have been. He (the Prime Minister) had then been fully convinced that the Home Secretary's offer of resignation had been unconditional and to take immediate effect. Under the circumstances, whether they were due to a misunderstanding or not, the public interest had compelled him to take at once a step of which he felt sure that his colleagues in the Government would approve. While no-one deplored more than he did the loss of so distinguished and able a colleague as Mr. Goldsmith, he felt that the present situation, involving not only the maintenance of order at home but our relations with a great and friendly Power, called for extraordinary action. He had accordingly put Sir John Naker, the Foreign Secretary, in temporary charge of the Home Office. It was, he knew, unusual for one Minister to hold both posts concurrently, but he felt that the circumstances justified this appointment.

There was a moment of stunned silence when Dr. Evans sat down, and then pandemonium broke out. The issue was twofold. There was first the insinuation against the police, which was generally felt to be unwarranted, and then there was the extraordinary initiative taken by the Prime Minister without full consultation with his colleagues. Member after member of the Opposition rose and attacked the Government on one or other of these points, and there were signs of mutiny among the Government supporters. Sir John Naker, in an ill-judged attempt to calm the tumult, announced that he had instituted an official inquiry into the affair at Leeds, and that, while the report received by the German Government had, he thought, been somewhat exaggerated, preliminary evidence tended to show that the police had exceeded their authority in dealing with the rioters.

This temporizing only served to exasperate the House still further, and provoked a split in the ranks of the Cabinet itself. Sir Willoughby Parker, K.C., then Minister for Agriculture, and an old enemy of Sir John Naker, flouted all precedent by asking his own Prime Minister whether he considered that the Foreign Secretary was a fit and proper person to conduct such an inquiry, and whether the matter was not one for a full debate. Dr. Evans was about to reply when he received a note passed to him from Sir John Naker. The House watched him in dead silence as he read it. Then the Prime Minister rose, and in a shaking voice pronounced the final death sentence on free parliamentary debate in the British Isles.

"I have just received information", he said, "that serious civil disturbances have again broken out in the North of England. In view of this fact and the unfinished character of the inquiry into the actions of the Leeds and West Riding police I do not think it expedient that this discussion should continue further at this time. Therefore, I propose immediately to advise the Council of Regency that this session of Parliament be suspended until further notice."

I shall not describe the scenes that ensued. The demise of the British Parliament was without order or dignity. The Council of Regency had, as I have already said, been hastily constituted as a shamefaced and temporary stopgap to fill the absence of the Crown. Its powers, although a legal commission was attempting to determine them, were still undefined. Their very vagueness made them the more formidable and the less easy to challenge. No-one knew whether the Prime Minister possessed the authority he claimed, but the Speaker, after a vain attempt to quell the uproar and even violence which arose, declared the sitting adjourned and left the House. Members gradually realized the futility of their indignation, and angrily dispersed. There was no Oath of the Tennis Court.

Attempts were made afterwards to prove that the Tyneside disturbances had actually begun at the time of the Prime Minister's announcement. But a few stormy meetings of the unemployed are all that can be adduced in support of this theory, and there is little doubt that the disorders to which he referred were fathered by the inventive brain of Sir John Naker, always ready to discover a quick exit from an embarrassing situation. Nevertheless, if these disorders were imaginary, they antedated the real thing by only a few hours. As the news of the Prime Minister's action was spread by Press and wireless all the latent anxiety and unrest came to a head, and the confusion in which Parliament had broken up Was the prelude to something little short of anarchy throughout the land.

The disorder occurred in two main areas—Tyneside and London. In the north the League of Britons had apparently lost much prestige as a result of the Leeds riot. Middle-class citizens who had been inclined to sympathize with its flamboyantly expressed ideals fought shy of their violent expression. But, although the movement thus lost much of its respectable fringe of adherents, it had also gained enormously in momentum. The cards were on the table, and, in the words of the Leaguers, "war had been declared on the alliance between Jewry and bureaucracy". Bureaucracy to the Leaguers meant the police.

The leaders of the movement did not lose sight of the confusion caused in high places by the German move, and seized their opportunity to stage another demonstration. This was to be a "battle march"—I detect Patrick Rosse's phraseology—through Newcastle, Jarrow and South Shields, three places which had for long before the war suffered from the worst kind of depression and unemployment, and after the brief armaments boom felt themselves slipping back into their former misery.

Like so many of Rosse's slogans the phrase "battle march" was vague but suggestive. The demonstration, which began in Newcastle as the usual affair of banners and brass bands, developed rapidly into a savage and semi-organized fight with the police. The authorities had their hands tied; already shaken by the questions which were being asked over the suppression of the Leeds affair, they now received a circular from the new Home Secretary warning them that on no account was popular feeling to be excited by the presence of large bodies of police or military. Nothing must be done which suggested persecution. Local forces were to deal with local disturbances.

The result was that the demonstrators found themselves from the first opposed by small bodies of police who, themselves affected by the indecision of their superiors, hesitated to take effective action and were quickly routed. As the mob saw the forces which represented discipline melt before it, its taste for triumph was whetted, and the next phase of the disorder was a series of deliberate attacks on police stations and assaults on isolated police units.

The marchers got no farther than Jarrow; here motor lorries and vans were commandeered, and the rioters circulated over a wide area of the poorer parts of Durham. In many places they were joined by parties of the younger unemployed, though it was noticed that the older, married men stood aloof. Everywhere small local police stations were attacked and looted, and in small villages the local constable's house was searched out and broken up. The police, wherever they could, resisted furiously, and would by now have acted without thought of future reprimands and inquiries, but the attack was so sudden and so widely dispersed that they had no time to form any effective concentration. Ten police officers were murdered by the rioters, and many others were man-handled and more or less seriously injured.

I have described the Durham disturbances from reports collected after the event, but I was myself a witness of part of the London trouble, and even I shudder as I remember what was for me the first spectacle of street anarchy, of open and destructive fury in men's faces, and the ugly snarl of a fighting crowd. I was working in my office in Fleet Street when O'Flynn, of the Irish United Press, which had premises across the passage, ran into my room. "Get your hat on if you want to see some fun," he said. "They say the boys are marching on Downing Street."

We chartered a taxi and reached Trafalgar Square, where we were stopped by a police cordon and got out. It appeared at first that O'Flynn was wrong. From inquiries in the crowd and from a large and friendly police constable I learnt that the square was the objective of the march, that Sir John Naker, apparently with the object of convincing the world and Germany that the Constitution had room for all sorts of politics, had authorized a mass meeting of the League in the Square, and that a procession was even then approaching down Haymarket.

The procession appeared in due course at the north-west corner of the square. It was led like so many London processions by a small detachment of mounted police, behind which marched a large and efficient brass band. As they came into the open the mounted police drew off to let the marchers defile into the area round Nelson's Column, but instead the brass band and the leading Leaguers advanced steadily down towards Cockspur Street and Whitehall. The police appeared momentarily nonplussed, and then, as the danger of the situation dawned on them, crossed the centre of the square at the trot and formed a weak cordon across Whitehall just below King Charles's statue.

Still the band came on, lustily playing "Hearts of Oak", and then the officer in charge of the mounted police made a grave mistake. Instead of falling back behind the strong reserve of foot police, which was now emerging from the region of the Admiralty Arch, he gave a sharp order, and drawing his long truncheon cantered forward with his men. They fell on the unfortunate bandsmen, who, hampered with their instruments, could put up no resistance and fell beneath the truncheon strokes as if pole-axed. Then the mass of the marchers behind lost their temper. They surged forward, grabbing at the truncheons and the feet of the mounted men, who became isolated and surrounded by the dense crowd. Two men disappeared from their horses, and at those points a hoarse and furious clamour arose above the general confusion, as the mob stamped and struck at something on the ground. The riderless horses reared and broke a way out through the crowd. One of them galloped round the square, skating and slipping on the smooth surface, and disappeared up St. Martin's Lane, where the crowd was relatively thin and fell back quickly as the frightened animal came towards it. The rest of the mounted police gradually fought their way out through the furious crowd down into Whitehall, where they were received into the ranks of a large body of police on foot which had now assembled to bar the way.

The crowd had tasted blood and was not to be held back. The numbers of the marchers were swollen by onlookers who found themselves infected by the mob-spirit. I saw a man near me forcing his way through the spectators, his face suffused with fury. He was cursing incoherently at the "blue bastards"; "Let me through: I'll get 'em!" he kept shouting. The bottleneck at the top of Whitehall became a confused mass of fighting men, but the police were in sufficient numbers this time, and had the advantage of organization. Their truncheons rose and fell mercilessly: one could hear from the steps of St. Martin's-in-the-Fields the sickening sound of the impact. But there was neither time nor room for quarter. At last the crowd began to give way, and those who had been bold to shout in the rear suddenly broke into hurried retreat as they saw the fighting zone approaching them. Similarly, as the leaders, engaged in fierce hand-to-hand fighting, noticed the pressure yield behind them, they felt that they were being abandoned and fell back in their turn to find supporters. The immediate battle was over, and I, who had been so far infected with the deadly spirit of the affair as to watch fascinated with my heart beating violently, now felt the chill of panic in the atmosphere and turned with those who stood beside me in hasty retreat. I had enough sense to leave the main streets for the by-ways running up to Covent Garden, and so escaped the headlong rout which swept up the Strand, with the mounted police, furious at the fate of their comrades, doing savage execution on the rearmost.

What I had seen was bad enough, but there was worse happening elsewhere in London. There was careful generalship behind the apparently disorderly outbreaks of the League, and the fight in Whitehall with its threat to the seat of Government was only a feint to distract the attention of the authorities. Simultaneously there were two savage outbursts against Jewry, one in Whitechapel and the other in Golders Green. In the East End armed gangs of roughs attacked the Jewish traders. Shop after shop was broken up and looted while their wretched owners were beaten, stripped naked and maltreated in various hideous ways. In Golders Green there was an organized assault on a social centre which had been started by Jewish philanthropists for the benefit of refugees during the war. After the place had been set on fire the affair developed into a manhunt, with scared old men and women as the quarry. My wife, who was out shopping in Hampstead, saw with bewilderment and horror a pasty-faced middle-aged Jew running full tilt down the main street with a hue and cry of Greyshirts tearing after him.

That same day Berlin, the hidden hand behind all this disorder, sent its first direct orders to Naker, and he obeyed. At midnight I was sitting by my wireless trying to collect European reactions to the doings of the day, when I suddenly heard Hamburg announcing an "important bulletin". It was addressed to "the people of Greater Germany" and it was as follows:

"The British Government is meeting with certain difficulties in controlling Jewish-organized anarchy which has occurred in every part of the country, and it has appealed for help to the Führer and Chancellor, in accordance with the obligations assumed under Article VI of the Treaty of St. James's. Adolf Hitler, whose mission, now as ever, is the maintenance of peace and good order, has decided therefore to dispatch a limited number of picked units of the Special Police to England to help in the work of restoring order to that country."

I sat motionless as the unctuous voice of the German announcer repeated his tidings, and during those seconds there flooded in upon me a full realization of the fate that had come upon us. The Treaty had been a shock and a portent, but the imagination had shrunk from envisaging its consequences. The rioting and the Government crisis had strained our nerves and demanded our attention, but it had been a day-to-day anxiety and had left little time to look ahead. Now I saw that these things were but as the chill wind that blows before the tempest, which at last had burst upon us. I will not say that at that time I foresaw all the horror and humiliation which was to come, but for one moment of vision I felt like a man standing on a hilltop and watching the shadow of a cloud sweeping across the land towards him. The last light of liberty was blotted out, and before me I could see nothing but darkness and terror. So I sat, and then the firelight and the familiar room came back to me, and I went to tell my wife the news.

It is said that the first Germans arrived at dawn, by air. How many there were of them has never been disclosed. They were not unduly conspicuous; one never saw them cantering on horseback along the principal streets, or standing, hand on holster, in the neighbourhood of the great railway stations. Yet anyone who had business with the C.I.D. or was concerned with the organizing of public assemblies would be sure to observe them standing in the background, taking notes; and public figures, in politics or industry, were apt to be politely questioned by them. But the surprising thing was that, beginning almost with the day of their arrival, the rioting lost its force, became sporadic, and at last gave way to an unnatural calm. It would not be right to say that the Greyshirt movement collapsed, but it became respectable. It marched now, but did not fight. When it beat up Jews and Socialists it did so with nice selectiveness, and calculated method. The Lord Mayor of London reviewed it. It formed a guard of honour for Professor Döppelganger, the great German authority on *Henry VI, Part I*, when he visited Stratford on the Birthday. It became almost as respectable as the British Legion.

Where, then, was Patrick Rosse? Was his passionate struggle over? A few parades, a little organized and cold-blooded cruelty—were these the marks of a Britain reborn? It is sad to admit it, but Rosse's doubts on these points were, for the time being, swiftly set at rest. Herr Meyer, joined now by a number of equally insistent *Parteigenossen*, firmly but gently took Rosse in hand. They waved cheque-books, and at the same time made suggestions. They took him to the Savoy, where many long dreams for the future might quiver in a golden haze of champagne—and many concessions might be granted for the immediate present. Rosse regained his self-respect in these surroundings, among the uniforms and pretty women; it was possible there to believe of Germany everything that Herr Meyer said; and political ideals, if they lost in precision, glowed splendidly in the distance. But the day of reckoning was coming, in his own heart, and Patrick Rosse knew it.

There were many other Meyers at work. On the day the German police arrived the B.B.C. lost its familiar voice, and gained a new one. The first news bulletin of the day consisted of a fulsome and rhetorical document extolling the new measure as an act of German friendship. There was no direct criticism of the British police—only a suggestion that they were at the moment overworked, and that the Germans were to act as temporary reinforcements—but citizens were urged to extend the hand of friendship towards the newcomers and to obey them implicitly. Thus, it was added, they would display the true spirit of order and discipline which was inherent in the British people but had been obscured by the "recent and unfortunate occurrences". The whole document, which was read in a non-committal monotone by an obviously unregenerate announcer, resembled a "pi-jaw" delivered to an unruly set of children by a schoolmaster who knew his own weakness. I do not know who had compiled it, but it was the voice of all that was left of the British Government.

The newspapers also had come under an iron hand. Comment on the measure was conspicuously absent. My message of the previous evening to New Zealand had just escaped the news censorship, but when I arrived at the office of the cable company that afternoon I found it was in full force. There was no ineffectual Foreign Office clerk to deal with this time. I was ushered straight into the presence of a genial and competent-looking Dr. Schultz, late, I was told, of the German passport control. He spoke a fluent if Teutonic English and firmly took charge of my copy, regretting the necessity with the appropriate and entirely *ersatz* charm. Would I be so kind as to wait while he read it?

I sat in some apprehension, for I had not minced matters, foolishly hoping that I would be able to get one last uncontrolled message through to my paper. Presently he looked up: "It seems you do not like the Germans, Mr. Fenton?" he remarked with a bland smile. I told him that I had no personal animosity, and that my message was intended entirely as an objective commentary on the situation. "Quite so," he replied, "but I am afraid that our friends in New Zealand might accidentally get a wrong impression from your words. If you please, you will keep your message to the facts, as the British Government has announced them. Perhaps you will revise it now? Here is a pencil."

He handed me back my copy, and I spent some minutes in a dead silence cutting it. He examined what I had left closely. "Splendid," he said, "and such a message is the better journalism, no?" I murmured something non-committal and turned to go. "One moment, if you please, Mr. Fenton," he said. "In future we will have the names and addresses of correspondents. It is more convenient so. Where do you live, please?" With misgivings I told him. "Thank you very much," were his parting words. "You will tell us if you change your home. I hope your English Mr. Billings, who is my opposite in Berlin, is received in a spirit so helpful. Good-bye, Mr. Fenton, and if you please more conservative messages in the future. Also be advised that journalists at present will send no private messages to their editors."

Fleet Street was simmering with suppressed fury. Representatives of the German authorities were ensconced in all newspaper offices with full credentials and virtual control of the news. Editors were warned that attempts to evade the censorship would result in confiscation of an issue or even the suspension of a newspaper. Journalists are always the best rumour-mongers, and the mere fact of the censorship had charged the air with electricity. The wildest stories were flying about, and, when the known facts were so fantastic, it was not difficult to believe the wildest. One report, which no one seemed to doubt, left me with an unpleasant sensation at the pit of my stomach. It was to the effect that a large mental hospital in North London had been inspected by the Germans for possible future use as a place of "protective custody".

Retribution had indeed been cruelly swift. The "new Europe" was Germany's, not ours. Within a month of the fatal treaty the great British Empire lay inert and inoperative, from the City of London, whence all financial confidence had flown, to the most distant of the outposts. In the Colonies authority was shaken, and isolated British officials feared for their lives. India, outside the neighbourhood of garrison towns, was given over to communal violence, and the tribes swooped down unresisted from the North-West Frontier. The Union of South Africa, through a *coup d'état*, became a republic, and formed its own independent alliance with Germany. My own New Zealand, with Canada and Australia, remained formally linked, as monarchies owning a common

King, but they began to look to America as their protector.

And in the heart of the Empire the canker was at work—high German officers at the War Office and the Admiralty, Nazi "experts" in all the industries, and certain of Himmler's policemen (not at first, perhaps, very many) who installed themselves in all the key points, and pored long over the records in Scotland Yard.

Chapter Four

STRANGE NUPTIALS

It was early in May that the German Embassy took over Bush House. "Bosche House" the Londoners called it; and stopped to stare every time they passed. No such portentous diplomatic establishment had been known before.

I don't remember how many rooms there were in that great skyscraper, but every one of them was occupied by Nazis enjoying full diplomatic immunity. Armed S.S. men in the vestibule paced up and down in front of a huge indicator which gave directions for reaching the Ambassador's Suite, the offices of the Military Mission, the Publicity Bureau, the Passport Control, the Sports Alliance headquarters, the Cultural Institute, and a number of other sections marked only by mysterious letters and figures. There was a constant stream of people going in and out; and Aldwych assumed as weighty and official an atmosphere as Whitehall. "Any more for the Seat of Government?" facetious bus conductors would sometimes ask at the stop at the bottom of Kingsway.

In the first week a giant housewarming party was given. It was no mere affair of the Diplomatic Circle; everyone of note in London life was invited. What is more, a large proportion went, explaining to their friends that they did so out of curiosity.

There was a nightmarish touch about the event. One's taxi moved slowly along the Strand, which was decorated for the occasion with Venetian masts bearing Swastikas and Union Jacks. The enormous Embassy was floodlit, and one surged into it beneath a gilt statue of Hitler, the Colossus of the modern world. Inside one was hustled from room to room, where a system of loudspeakers relayed Wagner and guttural greetings from across the North Sea. And all the while one kept meeting one's old English friends, and the familiar faces of the leaders of English life—faces known at Ascot, the Stock Exchange, and Church House, Westminster. People glanced at one another as contemporaries might be expected to do in the novel surroundings of the Day of Doom.

I found myself trapped in a corner with a broad-shouldered, keen-eyed Nazi Press official, a man named von Holtz, whom I knew and rather liked.

"Are you enjoying yourself, Mr. Fenton?" he asked. "It is splendid, is it not?"

I said I could understand that he thought it splendid, but added that I found it rather close.

"Come with me," he said. "I badly want to talk to you. I can take you on to the roof."

We escaped into a comparatively deserted corridor, and were soon climbing in the lift. Outside on the roof there was a pleasant breeze, just strong enough to give a slight motion to the folds of the huge Swastika flag. We leaned on the parapet, watching the lights of London and looking down the processional Strand to where Nelson stood on his column.

Von Holtz was the best kind of Nazi. It was an unpromising best, but he was not without ideals, reticences, and a dim respect for the world beyond Hitler's. He was old enough, and fortunate enough, to have inherited some traditions from the vanished Germany.

To-night he was happy, and could not stop talking of the grand "marriage feast" below. To him it was the symbol of a wonderful new alliance, by which the technique and spirit of British imperialism were to be forged by German *Kultur* into a weapon which was to rule the world, down to the last native in his hovel. It was a grotesque idea, but it was one which those Englishmen who were prepared to compromise with evil were beginning to formulate for themselves, if in rather different terms.

So von Holtz wanted to know particularly about some of the people who were at the reception. "Of course, we have them all fully card-indexed," he said, "but I would like to confirm some preliminary impressions." He whipped out a neatly multigraphed list of acceptances, carefully classified under such heads as "Society", "Universities", "Art and Literature". "Tell me," he said, "is this a good cross-section of the high officials of the Civil Service? And here, under Church, is it important that there is no representative of the Countess of Huntingdon's Connexion?" It appeared that every hundredth man in Burke's Landed Gentry not otherwise accounted for had been sent an invitation, and that but a small proportion of these people had come. ("Probably, they're too poor," I suggested, but he was not happy about the squires.) The pro-Nuremberg trade unions were fully represented, the economists had come in full force, and the City of London, von Holtz said, was "sound". But why were there so few novelists and painters, and why, please, had both H. G. Wells and Bernard Shaw, of whom so much had been expected, failed to turn up?

The list I found amusing, but it was a bore to take it too seriously. "Some people don't like parties," I said, and, though he thought this was frivolous, he reluctantly put his list away.

"At any rate," he said, smiling but very earnest, "you will agree that, apart from the Führer's coming visit, this is the most important event of the London Season? This, and the Nordic Games at Wembley."

I laughed. "I had not thought of it that way," I said, "I had not thought of a London Season. Why, there is no Court now, and many of the old rich and decorative people have gone abroad or are staying in the country. I don't think we can talk about a Season this year."

"Not, of course, in the old narrow sense," he replied, "but why should not London become a brilliant centre of art and intellect, directed to the service of the people and the State? There will be the German season at Covent Garden, and all the other forms of cultural exchange. A new vitality, a new sense of purpose will be given to your intellectual activities, and in this regeneration the present leaders of your cultural and even your social life have an undoubted part to play." Sublime in his racial conceit, he gazed over the twinkling West End. There was a note of wistfulness in his voice, and I rather wondered if he was looking for Mayfair and an invitation from a duchess. "London," he cried, "why should she not become the Vienna of the West?"

"And is Vienna so very brilliant?" I put in.

"The Führer has decreed that Vienna shall become eventually the cultural capital of the German Reich," he replied coldly. "And London——"

"Oh, and what has the Führer decreed for London?"

"The Führer believes that it is in London that yet new standards of pan-Nordic culture will be hammered out. It is a great task. Your fine traditionalism; our strength. Your forms; our spirit. What together cannot we do for civilization?"

He began to ask me whether I thought duelling was likely to become fashionable at Oxford and Cambridge. I felt I had heard enough.

"Look here," I said, "we know that in a military sense you Germans are now in a pretty strong position in Europe and the world, but there are limits to your power. At the moment it goes little farther than the point of your bayonets. It may be that one day you will be able to assert such a moral leadership that we shall all delight in following it, in our different ways. But meanwhile don't count too much either on the Countess of Huntingdon's Connexion or on the Society people who happen to have come to your party."

Von Holtz's friendliness, his naïveté, did not leave him, but a new grimness tightened the corners of his mouth. He made no reply, and I felt what an incredible fool he was, wedded to his crude idea of harnessing the whole life of England to Nazidom by the methods of the card-index. To tell the truth I was nettled, and I added with bombastic recklessness: "Those who think like you have a good deal of brute force at their disposal, but they cannot with brute force kill the soul of England."

Before I had finished speaking, I knew what he would reply. "The soul of England?" he said, "I don't insult you, I try to understand you. But was not the soul of England conquered, and made Nordic again, in the Great Blockade?"

At any rate von Holtz was right about the Season. At first it had an artificially stimulated life. Official entertaining (led by the German Ambassador himself, who leased the Superb for the purpose) was never on so lavish a scale. If the usual London hostesses were shy, their places were taken by a charming cohort of German ladies out of the Almanach de Gotha, whose parties, their guests declared, were of unexampled brilliance. The postponed opening of the Royal Academy was a disappointment, but it had been a bad year for artists, some of whose works, the circumspect ventured to say, were sadly "decadent". All who were expected to do so attended the Nordic League sports meetings, and there was a certain public excitement about the plan for the culminating Anglo-German Tattoo at Aldershot.

Von Holtz flitted about at such of these functions as his duties led him to attend with a joyful earnestness. He always had his multigraphed lists, and the card-index must have swollen considerably. I even met him at the Derby, which as a popular festival seemed as happy as ever, although there was but a thin show of fashion in the Paddock. But I don't think he was ever at a cricket match, and I often wondered if he had got down on any list the names of those members of the M.C.C. who still came up from the country to watch matches at Lord's, but went straight home again afterwards.

In general, what with the military missions and professorial exchanges, Germans were everywhere—in messrooms, senior common rooms and clubs. They did not, I am told, behave with conspicuous tact, but their very presence solved certain difficulties. In front of a German one was excused from saying what one thought about Hitler, the Grey shirts, and the policy of the Government.

About this time all sorts of familiar things quietly changed or disappeared. Anti-Hitler literature had long vanished from the bookshops, but now it was only with difficulty that one could buy the ordinary political writings of the pre-Nuremberg era. Churchmen ceased lecturing the politicians, and reverted to discussions on the nature of God. Most of the wealthy Jews had left just in time for America, taking their capital with them, and the British film industry collapsed in consequence. Many voluntary associations devoted to familiar causes held no meetings at all. Street oratory was forbidden, even at Hyde Park Corner. "Deutschland über Alles" followed "God Save the King" on public occasions. One or two great public schools failed to reopen after the Easter holidays, there were almost no worthy candidates for the I.C.S., and a Gilbert and Sullivan season at the Savoy was a failure.

Thus slowly the scene began to change, but against it the lives of ordinary people were, on the surface, very little altered. Troubles of work and wages, high prices and insecurity of employment, had been common since the war; they were not lessened, but neither were they yet much increased, by alliance with the enemy. The future was uncertain, indeed, bound up with all kinds of decisions that might be taken, not in London or Manchester, but in Berlin and Leipzig; but it was not the habit of Englishmen to peer far into the future. There were still moments of leisure and fun, and these could be enjoyed to the full. There was the romance of the lengthening spring evenings, a time for lovers, when the dullest suburb quivered with enchantment; there were the Sunday papers, sensational about non-essentials, to be read deliciously in bed; there were the pub, and the Oval, and dog-racing and fish-and-chips. All these could be enjoyed even if several of one's friends were joining the Greyshirts, and twice as many officials were busy at the town hall, and Sergeant O'Malley next door, of the local police, was scratching his head about the kind of report he must send in to the German inspector who had come to "co-operate". True, the picture-house was less attractive since there had been so many dull films that had to be fitted with "English sub-titles", and the music hall seemed to have lost all spontaneity, and the wireless, between the extremes of Beethoven and brass bands, was simply not worth listening to. But on the whole, if one was lucky and in work, life jogged on as before, and, Hitler or no Hitler, one could expect births, marriages and deaths, breakfast, dinner and tea.

So it seemed; but a little below the surface there were unmistakable signs that the common people were not spared the humiliation and the fears that haunted their leaders. The bar parlour of the "Sawyer's Arms", round the corner from where I lived, had once been a great place for discussing foreign politics. Everyone had had his views on what Hitler, Mussolini, Stalin, or Churchill were likely, or ought, to do next; and on most nights a friendly argument would develop, illustrated by head-shakings, scraps of private information, and expletives. Mr. Alf Stevens, a facile but dignified lawyer's clerk, would sum it all up towards closing time, and, by sheer force of personality, have his reading accepted as final. But after the Treaty he drank his beer in silence, there being no debate calling for his analysis. Soon not even the home news was discussed—it was merely explained, illustrated, and accepted. During Registration Week, for instance, there was a lot of talk about how various people fared at the town hall, but when a young stranger ventured to draw dark pictures of the uses to which the registration particulars might be put in the future no-one else did more than grunt, or throw darts with greater intensity. It was not to be long before a cell of the Greyshirts adopted the "Sawyer's Arms" as their headquarters, and Mr. Stevens and his boon companions were dispossessed of their red-plush cosiness. Perhaps they went to the "White Lion" farther down the street, but it was not their kind of place, and it is more likely that they drank bottled beer beside cheerless hearths at home. In either case, they must have preserved their latter-day silence, which was eloquent not so much of fear or foreboding as of a conviction that freedom of speech had suddenly become an empty privilege in England.

This queer silence, or, what was worse, a babble about indifferent things, descended in time on every honoured and popular institution. People went on doing the same things, but, it almost seemed, from new and depressing motives. My secretary, Smithers, was a pillar of North Street Congregational Church, Tanner's End, and once, before the war, he had persuaded me to give a talk on New Zealand to the debating society that was run in the schoolroom hard by. I spent a stimulating evening in the company of people who took life seriously, thought deeply within narrow limits, and had a strongly ethical approach to public affairs. Of the quality of their piety I was no judge, but it seemed to me that democracy at least was in no danger of senile decay while enough such earnest people were at hand to take humble parts in working it. The minister, over a farewell cup of cocoa, confessed that, with the introduction of conscription, pacifism was likely to become a big issue among his congregation. It was an admitted dilemma, when war and Fascism were regarded as equally abhorrent manifestations of evil; but to him the remedy in the human sphere was to go on working for conditions in which neither war nor Fascism could flourish.

It turned out, when war came, that there were only three determined conscientious objectors in the whole congregation. Smithers, who went off cheerfully with his class late in 1940, spoke of them without bitterness; but even at that stage I fancied he was a little less certain about his religious bearings. Back after Nuremberg, he resumed family life at Tanner's End, and it never occurred to me to ask him how his church was getting along. But one day some event of New Zealand interest took me to the neighbourhood, and I recognized the ugly group of buildings I had visited so long before. The notice board showed that my acquaintance, the Rev. M. Brownlow, was still pastor, and that Divine Service was still held at eleven and six-thirty on Sundays. But a great banner was flapping against the grimy Gothic windows, bearing an announcement quite out of keeping with my recollection of the practical Christianity of Mr. Brownlow and his flock. It said that the subject of the sermon next Sunday evening was "Will the Second Coming be next year?"

I asked Smithers about this, at the first opportunity. "Yes," he said, "things are different now at North Street. Our congregations are no smaller, and we sing the same hymns and hear much the same prayers. But you could hardly call us Radicals to-day. Some of us are still great admirers of Dr. Evans, but Mr. Brownlow says that in the past we have tended to identify the Gospel too much with some particular programme of social reform. He says that it is time to lay more emphasis on personal holiness. Some of us don't care much for the Apocalyptic teaching he goes in for nowadays, but others do. I believe the Church means more to us to-day than it ever did."

"And the debating society?" I asked. "Oh," he said, "we

use the schoolroom on Wednesday nights for a prayer-meeting."

So much for the democratic spirit, as nurtured by faith. Just as the fiery Socialists had become Greyshirts, or were simply disillusioned, so the more bourgeois Radicals were taking refuge in a purely personal religion. Henceforth, from bus tops I looked with special interest at the blank façades of Nonconformist chapels. I took them to be the monasteries in which frustrated democrats found, I hoped, a true consolation.

But what of the worldlings in positions of greater influence, who bore a much heavier responsibility for the tragedy of the age? Some of them, as I have said, gyrated, gaily or desperately, in the inner circle of Herr von Holtz's London Season. They were the simple turncoats, into the workings of whose minds it would be unprofitable to enter. But there were several thousand others who had supported the elaborate superstructure of English life, who had been tricked or not, as it might be, into approval of the Peace of Nuremberg, and who remained loyal at heart to the old standards and the old ideals. These were the Army men, the original Civil Servants, the dons, the leaders of local industry up and down the provinces, the country gentlemen—in short, that great body of Englishmen who, more truly than most of their fellows, had what I might call a moral stake in the old order. These were the greatest sufferers in mind and spirit. It was not only that many of them had the intelligence to see that their own future, and that of their children, was barren and perhaps painful; it was that they knew they had been doorkeepers in the Temple while the Ark, by stratagem, had been defiled.

Their human consolations were a mockery.

Where the land is dim from Tyranny
There tiny pleasures occupy the place
Of glories and of duties.

They had the opportunity to approach that brittle, unreal world that represented "modern thought" in London. They could listen every day to the hypocrisy of the Nurembergers in high places, to the twittering exponents of "neo-Fascism" and "neo-Teutonism". It was only to them to follow the neurotics of Mayfair and "go Viennese", as a self-deceptive preliminary to "going Prussian". But mostly they preferred to do what remained of their business quietly, and then to go home or to the club to talk absently of unimportant things, or play bridge. Every turn of the day brought them against some fact, some symbol, some situation that put them in mind too poignantly either of the world that was passing away or of the world that was being born.

Humour saved many immediate situations, but Mr. Punch was already a peace casualty. Reminiscence satisfied the very old, and dissipation attracted the young. In some circles there was a short phase of *fin de siècle* nastiness which was heaven-sent material for Dr. Goebbels. Much worse, there was a loosening of the moral fibre in almost all places where the example should have been set. There were, of course, countless splendid people who maintained their own integrity, but even they learnt to be suspicious of others. Peculation reared its head where it was undreamt of before—in local government, in Whitehall itself. Crimes of violence increased. "We have cut ourselves off from nearly all our traditions," a penetrating friend of mine remarked, "and so we have to start again from the moral level of the Balkans." In fact we had become familiar with the spiritual atrophy of Nazism before we had submitted to its discipline.

Such was the England awaiting Herr Hitler. He might well have come as arranged in the last week of May. He might well have been satisfied to look down on distracted London from the roof of Bush House, while the plane-trees were in young leaf, and murmur: "I had no idea it was so beautiful." But bigger changes were on the way, and he was patiently awaiting them. One by one, as spring melted into a golden summer, his policemen stepped confidently ashore at Harwich and Gravesend.

Chapter Five

A LIGHT THAT FAILED

HITLER paused, and by his own standards he was right. The fruit even now was trembling on its rotting stalk; let God, or some other agency, blow, and it would inevitably fall into his lap. Time, he must have thought, was his almost fanatical ally.

Yet can it be that Hitler's was not the ultimate wisdom? Is it "wishful thinking" that makes one hark back already to those lines of Tennyson's that people used to quote complacently about the Finns, about the "banked-up fire" which even a hopeless fight for freedom will leave glowing for future deliverance? For in those brief despairing months there was at least one spark of determined heroism in England, which even grew into a tiny flame. Hitler came and quenched it—how easily! . . . but not, perhaps, for ever.

It is with diffidence, almost with shame, that I write of my acquaintance with Stephen Mallory in those days. He never openly summoned me; but I know in my heart that he represented a challenge which I had not the courage to accept. I had a thousand excuses, of course, as we all did, including the bravest of us. I was a New Zealander; I was a mere journalist, not supposed to mix in politics; I had my wife and child to consider; I had few gifts to place at his disposal; and in any case, since it was impossible to resist the trend of history, one must try to adapt oneself to it. I knew that these were only excuses, and he knew that I knew it. But he said nothing; because he was finding just the same moral cowardice among men who had gaily gone off to France three years before, quite ready to lay down their lives for freedom.

Mallory has not yet emerged as a figure in history. He had no chance to lead an active revolt behind the barricades. To the Nazis he was an obscure agitator, soon put out of the way. To newspaper readers only his death was remarkable, and even that, alas, would not have seemed so a couple of months later. But to those Englishmen who, silently, came under his ever-widening influence he stands as an inspiration as well as a reproach, and one of the last things I recall before I was expelled the country is his name chalked boldly, under cover of night, on the railway arches of Limehouse.

Stephen Mallory. Wild hope suggests that the name may one day be a war-cry, and a triumphant one. It is whispered to-day in gaols and concentration camps, and wherever two or three are gathered together in the name of freedom. It is sometimes shouted by those about to die.

No doubt a legend has already grown up round it. Deeds, I expect, are attributed to Mallory which he never did, or could have done. Yet the legend does but express his significance to British patriots, which is profound. A country has no claim to resurrection if, with its political forms, its spirit too has entirely perished; but the memory of Mallory, and of the little band of heroes he inspired, may be enough to ensure the spiritual survival of England.

It was a spiritual battle he fought. The joy of grasping material weapons and making a last heroic stand against the oppressor was not his. He had not the rude task of a Hereward the Wake; indeed, I doubt if he was fitted for it. The foes he fought were moral evils, in and around him, and, as we have seen, they advanced with a rapidity and insidiousness which paralysed most of his countrymen. But he did not give in, and it was the smallest of his fears that his struggle would be ended, like that of fighters on a humbler plane, by a German bullet.

Mallory, it must be confessed, was no democrat. Rather, he was *fascigeant,* believing that Britain, suddenly finding herself plunged into such a state of shame and self-pity as marked the Weimar Republic, needed the counterpart of the National Socialist movement to restore her self-respect. But it was a Christian Fascism that he envisaged, a movement that would redeem the pagan brutality of Hitler's régime, and set forth as its first principle a respect for the rights of others. He saw the very shame of Britain as a likely foundation for this purified nationalism. There was to be no talk of stabs in the back, of international Jewish machinations, or of a gallant war lost on the home front. To the moral surrender the whole country had been party, the people as well as the leaders. No-one was to blame but ourselves; and the rearmament we needed was "moral rearmament", though that phrase had been emasculated by a pseudo-religious revival much advertised before the war began. To this end Mallory would have adapted some of the methods of the Nazis and the Greyshirts, as General Booth captured from the devil the good tunes. He had thoughts of red shirts, like Garibaldi's, and he believed in his heart in the Party-State. But no-one troubled to assess him as a candidate for the job of Dictator of Britain, and no-one paid the least attention to his theories, which were based on some half-forgotten reading in political science at Cambridge. It was simply his burning patriotism which made those who came in contact with him uncomfortable, ashamed, or, in a few cases, resolved to fight and die for freedom. Nor did his theories matter. The immediate and belated task was to "stop the rot", and persuade people that all was not yet lost.

Mallory was less than forty years of age. He stooped slightly, had lank, black hair, and sharp features that were not too prepossessing. It was, however, impossible to deny the lively brilliance of his eyes. He had had a distinguished academic career, had been called to the Bar, and had published an authoritative work on the economics of the steel industry. Rich and well-connected, he had soon found his way into the House of Commons, where he had sat under the quaint banner of National Labour. But he never made his mark in Parliament, for he was an indifferent orator. He had been connected with a number of societies whose aim included a more determined effort at economic planning. He had been useful, during the war, at the Ministry of Supply, though, if the doctors had let him, he would have enlisted.

He opposed the Peace of Nuremberg, and crossed, with a crowd of others, the floor of the House. But in the months that followed he busied himself with plans of Anglo-German economic co-operation; and the hopelessness of it all must have been borne upon him only by degrees. At any rate, it was some time before he settled down as a confirmed critic of the Government's foreign policy, acquiring the art of the Supplementary Question, and spoiling a good deal of Sir John Naker's fun. Not until the Treaty of St. James's was signed did he look around him and realize, with sickening force, that among the debaters and the arguers, the elder statesmen and those who cried "Ichabod", he alone, apparently, had received the call to win the British people back to the responsibilities of nationhood. And this, he knew, was not a matter of asking questions in Parliament.

I first made his acquaintance early in June, when Australia and New Zealand began a tentative approach towards the United States. He sought me out and invited me to lunch at the Reform Club. He wanted to know more about feeling in the Antipodes than the controlled Press could tell him, and he asked me what would be the effect on opinion there if the United Kingdom were ever to renounce her alliance with Germany and face up to the consequences, whatever they might be. The most outspoken anti-German had never before, in my hearing, done more than suggest resistance to further Nazi encroachments, and I sat back in surprise. "The effect", I could only say, "might be magical, but so would the cause." "No," he said. "I am quite serious. It would surely not be miraculous if England were to exert her utmost efforts to throw off a foreign tyranny. Even now there is time."

One night a little later he outlined his plan in greater detail to a party of us gathered in his chambers in the Temple. A strong Government was to proclaim martial law, disband the Grey shirts, and put an end once and for all to the deliberate German-fomented attacks on Jews and Socialists. If necessary, this was to be done with machine-guns. Properly executed, the manœuvre might throw the Germans off their balance. They might hesitate and threaten, and in the meantime the second part of the plan could be brought into operation.

The Navy was intact and so was the small Regular Army of 200,000 men. They should be adequate for the immediate defence of the country from actual invasion, even though the German military missions now knew their organization from A to Z. The real danger was from the air, and here we must rely mainly on passive defence. The air-raid shelters were still in existence, for the preservation of human life, and until the system of wardens could be re-established the police could take over the responsibility of the A.R.P. It took time for air attacks to do any irreparable damage to a country's organization; and if we made up our mind to it we could proceed quite calmly to this second part of the plan.

"And what, then, is the second part of the plan?" I asked.

"Simply", he said, "to deport, imprison, or shoot every German policeman in England.

"Then", he went on, "the struggle begins and grows. Say what you like, the world would be in the melting-pot again. Canada would be back in the fray once more—what, in such circumstances, could hold her back? The spectacle of such a gallant last-minute fight would grip the world; I think we should hear no more of a revolution in India. And what of the United States? Goebbels has already been foolish enough to show the beginnings of an anti-American Press campaign, and to talk mysteriously of the combined might of the British and German navies. America must see that this is her last chance as well as ours. And so is it Italy's, and Turkey's, and Scandinavia's. Since the overthrow of Stalin there is no chance of a new German-Russian alliance. Once overcome the initial difficulties, and the rest would be easy."

Mallory always grew excited as he pictured the pieces of a jigsaw world thus neatly falling into place again. But it was not the mechanics of anti-Nazism that excited him, it was the passion and faith that must first lie behind it. He did not want another war about a map; he wanted to uncover again the underlying moral pattern of human society, which no tyranny could permanently disperse. Ways and means, he thought, lay always at the disposal of a resolute will; and there was an inner rottenness in Hitlerism which would cause its swollen bulk to begin to disintegrate as soon as it was met, at any point, with a determined resistance. The immediate problem was not military or political; as he put it: "If God grants us the courage to raise the sword He will teach us how to wield it."

Mallory looked eagerly around the group—composed of some of the unconverted whose loyalty and discretion were unquestioned but whose determination and courage were not.

By this time, as I knew, he had formed the nucleus of his movement—a score of men of various callings who were all now busily at work, as he was, preaching the gospel of national self-help. He called them merely Patriots; he formed no party and collected no funds. One of his theories was that of the Fascist Party-State inverted; at the ultimate crisis, he believed, a nation could save itself only by the spontaneous functioning of its natural parts. Given an army and a police force, a civil administration and a labour movement still intact, whose leaders believed in the national cause and could communicate their faith to the rank and file, then, he said, the merest word from some central rallying point would be enough to start the struggle with every chance of success. There were historical instances of this, which Mallory was fond of citing—the Risorgimento, Primo de Rivera in Spain, or (a perverted example) the rise of Hitler himself—and in each of these the inner conviction of the patriots, and not their strategical situation, was the deciding factor. It was morally impossible, according to Mallory, for the largest imaginable foreign force to hold down an unwilling and determined Britain.

Against this theory someone instanced the apparent powerlessness of the Czechs, who, of all Hitler's victims, had the reputation of professing the fiercest patriotism. There were the Poles, too, who had preserved their proud national spirit for centuries, without ever succeeding in building a durable State. There were the Finns, who fought the hardest in defence of their freedom, but gave way in the end; and there were the Austrians and the Danes, whose cultural achievements on the fringe of Germania had shown what a purified Teutonism could become, but who had been conquered in a day. The methods of the Gestapo seemed unchallengeable.

"Only because they have never been challenged," replied Mallory. "The neighbours of Germany, however great their courage and national pride, have always acknowledged a kind of divine right of German arms. The huge German race was dominant in Central Europe long before it achieved political unity; and this dominance found mystical expression in the theoretical Holy Roman Empire. The surrounding races were part of the German scheme of things, and if that scheme came to involve the establishment, by violence and cruelty, of an immense *Mitteleuropa*, they felt in their hearts that they must ultimately submit to it. But with ourselves, it is different. We are outside the German system, and we have imperial traditions of our own. Just as Germany is indestructible, so are we. The presence of German policemen on British soil is an aberration of history so monstrous that the smallest effort of will could put an end to it—that is the first thing. But we also have our responsibilities on the Continent, counterbalancing those of Germany. After the war is resumed and won we must see to it that the vassalage of Germany's neighbours becomes an honourable and creditable one again, working for the good of civilization as a whole."

Mallory was no League of Nations man, or abstract political thinker. He divided the weak from the strong, and knew his *Lebensräume*. He was not poles apart from the Fascists, and had once contributed an article to Mosley's *Action*. In the early days of the Hitler régime, had he had the direction of British foreign policy, he would have gone far to strike a bargain with Germany over respective spheres of influence on the Continent and overseas. He would almost certainly have been accused of belonging to the "Cliveden Set"; and he would not have admitted, until it was proved up to the hilt, that it was both useless and immoral to negotiate with the Nazis. But the time arrived when his conscience spoke, with the single voice of patriotism and Christian justice. Like many others, he came to realize the error of Nuremberg, but, unlike them, he did not despair. He still believed in the politics of power, but he thought the power was as much in British as in German hands. It was latent, but it was there; and it lay in the spirit of the race, co-existent with the race itself, which any resolute political engineer could transform into successful action.

Much of this seemed to us pretentious nonsense, like Hitler's or Rosenberg's; but it is impossible to fight a war without some suspension of disbelief in fallacies about race. Mallory's best claim on our credulity was that none but he made any attempt to rally us in the defence of the things which in past times we had held dear. At the least, it was surely better to fight for a lost cause than to own no cause at all.

Mallory, then, set himself to fan back into a flame the damped-down embers of British patriotism; and he would have hit more than the headlines had his little bellows produced anything but the tiniest flicker. But, alas, he failed, or seemed in his lifetime to have failed; and the world, which he wished to save, has still largely not heard of him. He was not a conspirator, but a prophet; and as a prophet he was first unheard, and then, almost casually, silenced. But he never himself abandoned hope, or recoiled for long before his successive disappointments. He died believing that he had started a movement that would sweep on to victory. In the realm of political thought, and in the long run, perhaps he had.

The former War Coalition had by this time become sadly disorganized. Mallory went to see all the old leaders, whose voices, not long since, had been heard on the wireless exhorting the nation to fight on to the end. They received him, I believe, without enthusiasm, and when he had gone forgot about him, unless they wondered whether he was an *agent provocateur*. Most of them had already retired from political life. They were lost without their Parliamentary soundingboard, their privileges and their nice rules of procedure; they could hardly be expected, at their age, to take leading parts in the Continental melodrama that now dominated English politics, with its private armies, and strange disappearances, and multitude of spies. "We have lived too long," was the burden of their complaint, and, as they had played out the game honourably according to the rules, they were entitled to excuse themselves thus. From many a remote country house, its gardens falling somewhat into neglect, Mallory drove despondently back to the village station—not always unnoticed by a man in a high peaked cap lounging near the lodge gates.

But these lost leaders had sons: were they not picking up the dropped torch? Alas, in their bewilderment, their judgment seemed to desert them. Some of them were frankly with Rosse, irrelevantly hunting the Jews; others responded to Mallory's approaches with futile plans for minor *coups d'état*. A small proportion, who might have passed as honourable men in simpler circumstances, were already making their contacts with the German party bosses—giving mixed house parties at home or lending aristocratic tone to the orgies in the Karinhalle. The great majority were helpless and dismayed, waiting to see what would happen next—ready, perhaps, to strike a simple blow for freedom as part of a disciplined revolt, but unable to plan or lead it.

One of Mallory's group was a young and not unsuccessful stockbroker. This Mr. C. (his name is better not given, as the Nazis may still have failed to track him down) used to tell some incredible stories about conditions in the City. "We are business men, not politicians," was the common slogan among those who in other circumstances might have found it useful to become Conservative M.P.s, and this asseveration covered a multitude of strange dealings which trailed the Red Ensign in the dust. The financial outlook was, of course, as black and uncertain as it could well be, and the whole of British foreign trade was in the balance. There was a big field for speculation, and some cause for panic. One fact alone was certain, and that was that the political power in the shade of which financial power must wax or wane lay on the other side of the North Sea. The central finances of the British Empire were already at the disposal of German development in south-east Europe. Dr. Schacht was made an honorary member of the Court of the Bank of England, and it was astonishing how many heel-clicking Nazis were entertained in the battle-scarred halls of the Liveries. C. was decided on this point—it was quite impossible to finance a national revolution in the City of London.

But it was not so much money that was wanted as influence. What then of the various organs of publicity that a short while ago had been loudly urging on the war effort? The Ministry of Information itself was of course part of the Government machine, which meant that it was entirely at the disposal of the Nazis. They had increased its technical efficiency, and imported into British public life all those devices of propaganda which, crude as they seem to those outside its range, are effective enough on the mark. The wartime heads had long ago resigned, with the better part of their staff, but the vacant places were soon filled with "advisers" from Germany, who knew what they were about. During the war German propaganda had set out to disturb and depress us. It had succeeded, and now a new technique was required. We were to be calmed, reassured, mildly convinced. How skilfully it was done! Every Briton has by this time a deep track in his subconscious mind scored by those endless posters showing the combined might of the British and German empires, busts of Shakespeare and Goethe entwined with laurel leaves, showing, above all, a British and a German workman generously shaking hands and saying, "*Nicht wieder* —never again.*"* There is something hypnotic about pictures of workers shaking hands.

The Alliance propaganda was not confined to posters,. It penetrated every activity of life, and rapidly built up that clever picture, too soon shown to be a dissolving view, of a sort of Viennese honeymoon for Nazidom and its British bride. A painfully forced smile as of that lost easy-going Austria came over the countenances of our cultural invaders; for a brief moment it was Lilac Time. We waltzed, drank duty-free hock, and bought splendid books with baroque title-pages. Strength-through-Joy offered the British worker such tours of the Black Forest as the Polytechnic could never accomplish. The rubber truncheon was for the moment hidden away.

On the crest of such a wave even Lord Haw-Haw could rise with all his old sublimity. He was now installed in Broadcasting House, whence he lulled the listening public into a belief in a serene and happy future that was being prepared for them behind the scene. At first people were inclined to laugh at him, and the Mallory group rejoiced that the Nazis had made such a psychological blunder as to send him over. But he began to say so many of the nice things which people wanted to believe that it was not long before one ventured to remark, in suburban sitting-rooms, that perhaps he was not such a bad fellow after all. Nevertheless, he went everywhere with an armed escort; and, somewhat later than the time of which I am writing, as he was hurrying across to a taxi in Portland Place, a young Guards officer was thought to have aimed a revolver at him. The officer was shot dead by the Nazi escort; it was the first and almost the only "unpleasantness" of the kind, and it was hushed up.

Here, then, was a formidable barrier to Mallory's propaganda campaign. It was difficult to see any way through or round it. The Press was still nominally free, except that it was forbidden to criticize German institutions, but it had abdicated from the leadership of public opinion. Reuter was nationalized. The most influential newspapers had gone; one does not spend twopence a day to read of prophecies belied or fulfilled. The big provincial dailies gave up national politics, and turned to local and sectional interests. The popular dailies, deserted by nervous advertisers, were swamped by Dr. Goebbels's *People's Observer*, which, though supposed to be a kind of London edition of the *Völkischer Beobachter*, provided the unthinking Briton with such an attractive substitute for *Picture Post*, the *Mirror*, and the *Express* as no Berliner had ever seen. Some of my Fleet Street acquaintances took jobs on this monstrosity, explaining, of course, that "they were interested in it only from a technical point of view", in its pictures, or racing news, or dramatic criticism. They were careful to steer clear of Mallory.

At one time I suspected Mallory of plotting a desperate revolt with his friends on the British General Staff, with whom he had some very secret contacts, or even of trying to shame the leaders of the Greyshirts into biting the vile hand that fed them. But he stuck to his view that the first preparations for such a move were moral and psychological, and for this he pinned his remaining hopes on the world of labour. He persuaded himself that if the solid basis of British society was firm it mattered not that the superstructure was breaking. He paid a visit to Transport House. When he returned he was very nearly in despair.

"My God, Fenton," he said, "the British trade-union movement has crumpled at the mere raised fist of Dr. Ley. D. told me there had been some changes in the Executive, but there is a completely new crowd there now. That's the devil about this controlled Press. A man like Citrine can have the whole of his life's work bullied or bribed out of existence, and then not know how to get the facts before the workers or the public.

"Well, they are a strange, hunted lot at Transport House now. A rather pansy young man who had obviously never done a day's manual work in his life seemed to regard me as an envoy of doomed Jewish capitalism.' The British worker is done with fighting your battles,' he said. I asked him if he was old enough to remember what had happened to the trade unions in Germany. He said that when capitalism was destroyed in Germany the trade unions turned to fulfil a more constructive function, and that we must be ready for the same glorious revolution over here—not without the cooperation of the Communists. Isn't it extraordinary how, with big guns and determination, Hitler has been able to turn all the old political theories upside down?"

Next day Mallory went back to his old constituency in Lancashire. I saw him off at Euston, feeling acutely that his failure was due in the long run to the cowardly inactivity of such as I. I muttered over again my feeble self-justifications; and when the whistle blew I felt like jumping into the compartment with him, without quite knowing why. He pushed me back on to the platform with a melancholy smile.

Three weeks later I heard from him, at the "Old Red Lion", Oldham. "How glad I am I have come back here," he wrote. "This is where our resistance begins. You could sweep the whole decadent world of London away to-morrow, and these people would throw up a new set of politicians and financiers and professors without any fuss at all. I have been addressing some meetings of the local Cotton Spinners' Association, and, if the men here are typical of the rank and file of the trade-union movement up and down the country, I can assure you that next September's meeting of the T.U.C. will change the whole situation. The Greyshirts are strong here too, but I prefer the quiet strength of the loyal Labour men. No Hitler could begin to undermine their confidence and determination, or could resist them when the time comes to act."

I had two or three letters from Mallory after that. He spoke of meetings and processions, and admitted to some unprofitable street encounters with the Greyshirts. There was something of the demagogue about him after all; he must have thumped the tub good and hard. Some of his friends shared with him a tour of all the industrial regions; nowhere was their belief shaken in the nationalist fervour of the British working man or in the crucial importance of the next Trades Union Congress.

He was, on a short view, deceived. History records that this Congress never met. It records very little (as yet) about Mallory and his movement. In the remaining London papers there was only this, an agency message published on Monday, 23rd June:

"In a slight street disturbance in Oldham market-place on Saturday evening an unfortunate accident caused the death of Mr. Stephen Mallory, of Crown Court, Temple, E.C., a former National Labour M.P. for the borough. Mr. Mallory was wounded in the head by a revolver bullet which is thought to have been fired inadvertently by one of the Socialist demonstrators.

"Mr. Mallory, who was thirty-eight and unmarried, had been staying at Oldham for some time. He served in the Ministry of Supply during the last war, but for some time had retired from political life.

"The street disturbance was of a minor character, and Major Robinson, the newly-appointed Chief Constable of Oldham, states that order has now been permanently restored. 'We have had some trouble lately with Socialist agitators,' he told a Press Association representative yesterday, 'but we are taking firm steps to preserve law and order. A detachment of Greyshirts rendered yeoman service in giving immediate assistance to the police, and I cannot be sufficiently grateful for the help given by those members of the German police who are here under the exchange system, commanded by the gallant Captain Trauber.'"

Many people read this item of news and blenched, or hung their heads with shame, but there were few comments on it. At the inquest they brought in a verdict of accidental death; but from evidence as reported in the *Oldham Chronicle* it would not have taken Lord Peter Wimsey to deduce that of all the unhappy people huddled together in the market-place that Saturday evening the only man likely to be armed with a revolver was the gallant Captain Trauber himself. He soon became Major Trauber, and got himself appointed to a coveted post (for such as he) in Whitechapel.

After that, one heard no more of the Patriots—if, indeed,

one had heard of them before. A bullet from a minor Nazi gangster brought that whole grandiose movement to an end. One or two younger men, hitherto known to have been somewhat active on the fringe of public life, disappeared, apparently to the complete mystification of the police. One day, when it is quite certain that they are either dead or safe from Nazi clutches, I will write what I know about them. Meanwhile, I must confess that I had certain fears for my own safety, though Heaven knows I am no hero, and had done nothing to deserve the crown of martyrdom.

I expect that by this time the mill-owners of Oldham, hot under the collar when the Nazi "labour leaders" order them about their business or whisk their plant off to Chemnitz, have long forgotten the Mallory "incident", and have never known that he might have been their saviour. Others, like myself, are vainly trying to forget him, recalling that we had declined to join him, not out of an intellectual disbelief in his chances of success, but out of the moral paralysis which, the punishment of those who put their hand to the plough and then look back, had descended upon the whole of our generation. Himmler may have it in his secret records somewhere that a not very dangerous centre of resistance was, as a measure of extreme precaution, neatly liquidated during June. The failure of Stephen Mallory—Stephen the Protomartyr—was, you may say, complete.

Yet indeed the banner of freedom had been raised, however hopelessly. There had at least been that little demonstration on the windy market-place at Oldham. Lancashire men had shouted their belief in freedom, and Lancashire hearts had beat high, for a moment. A small group of patriots had staked everything for the salvation of England. In the general disorderly retreat a token challenge had been made.

I suspect that Adolf Hitler, who has a flair for these things, was about the only man who at that time accorded Mallory his full importance. I believe he watched the small affair at Oldham with considerable anxiety. He knew well how a political snowball can start to roll; he knew the illimitable possibilities of audacity and faith. Even with Mallory out of the way he must have decided to take no chances.

The inevitable next step followed swiftly. Its cue, however, was given not by any internal development, but, to the surprise of everyone, by the President of the United States.

It was known that Washington had serious misgivings over the turn of events. Then, just a week after the light of Mallory had been put out, the President chose the occasion of a meeting of the Pan-American Conference for an important statement of American policy. He referred bluntly to the German "domination" of Great Britain, and said that Americans' worst fears were being fulfilled. The American Government, he said, saw with concern the effect which this domination would have on the policy of the United Kingdom. The danger of a penetration of German ideas and German power into the western hemisphere was imminent. He then touched on the position of the British Dominions and colonies. He reaffirmed that the existing Monroe doctrine covered Canada, and that no new influence on the policy of that great country could be permitted by the United States. The ensuing passage of his speech, so fraught with immediate and indirect consequences, is worth quoting.

"The Monroe doctrine," said the President, "like all great political conceptions, is elastic in character and expands itself to embrace new developments in human thought and human history. It was originally evolved to preserve the stability of the American Continent, and to safeguard the life and freedom of those States which have their home and being on the soil of that continent. The basic idea inspiring it was the preservation of peace and the *status quo* within a wide area of the globe. With the vast development of communications and the evolution of new and long-range weapons during the past half-century, can we doubt that the area of the earth's surface necessary for the free and unhampered growth of the American peoples has not also expanded? Can we doubt that if the sovereignty and integrity of such vigorous and prosperous young nations as Australia and New Zealand were threatened, this would not also be a threat to the safety and freedom of every denizen of the western hemisphere? The Monroe doctrine has ceased to have a merely American significance."

The President's words were received in the United States with surprisingly unanimous approval: they were received in Germany with a revealing burst of fury. The indignation which Dr. Goebbels and his men felt on behalf of the British Empire resembled the screech of a vulture which had seen someone attempting to revive what it had regarded as its own legitimate carrion. We were told, till we yawned, of this brutal and unprovoked threat to our national sovereignty. The Propaganda Ministry in Berlin had for long been deprived of a worthy target for its abuse, and it fell on "American imperialism" and the "American lust for world domination" with renewed ardour.

Gradually this clamour developed into a new expression of policy. The German people, it was declared, would not stand by and see their allies despoiled by robber Powers. The

American menace had welded the German and the British peoples into a new and closer unity, and had given them a new mission, the protection of the "Nordic peoples" all over the world. Finally it was announced, with a bray of trumpets, that the Führer himself would set the seal of this new brotherhood by vouchsafing his presence on English soil. The oppressed British should have a chance of welcoming their new Protector in person, and it was to be a very different affair than the "State visit" mentioned at the time the Treaty was signed.

There is reason to believe that the decision to visit Great Britain was Hitler's own, and was taken against the advice of his lieutenants, who feared that his presence might be a stimulus to any lingering tendencies towards independence. But the Führer saw himself now as a demi-god indeed, and no longer felt the need to retire to his eyrie in the Bavarian Alps in order to experience his godhead. The old lion had been cowed into submission, and he, the tamer, would now strut into the cage in full uniform, and make it go through its newly learnt tricks, to the crack of the whip.

Göring and Ribbentrop acquiesced, but they were taking no chances. There should be loaded rifles, as well as a whip, to ensure that nothing untoward befell the lion-tamer. Hitler, it was announced, would arrive on 1st July, but the "Führer's Bodyguard" would precede him. Owing to the censorship and the general atmosphere of secrecy which now enveloped everything it was never known how many men constituted Hitler's bodyguard on this occasion, but, according to a rumour emanating from Hull, 20,000 men were landed at that port alone from troopships during the week before the coming of the Führer. They were not seen in London, however, except as small detachments of superlatively well-disciplined men, who were apparently quartered in the Guards' Barracks in Birdcage Walk. Even so, public attention was carefully distracted from their presence by the loudly heralded arrival of several thousands of Hitler Youth, on a mission of *Kameradschaft*. They were to take part in the festivities, and subsequently were to propagate the doctrines and ideals of Nordic boyhood throughout the schools of Great Britain. These youngsters, after arriving in *Kraft durch Freude* vessels at Tilbury, paraded through Central London and were given a mayoral banquet at Guildhall, before being quartered on families in the suburbs. They seemed to have plenty of pocket-money, and were seen everywhere in the streets during the latter part of June.

Hitler's entry into London was superbly staged, and even

the weather was subservient The *Scharnhorst*, with an escort of German and British destroyers, arrived in the Thames soon after eleven o'clock. Opposite Greenwich the Führer entered a motor-torpedo boat and proceeded up river, accompanied by six similar craft flying the Swastika flag from the bows and all manned with rigidly watchful S.S. men facing the banks with machine guns at the ready. Tower Bridge, with elephantine courtesy, broke its lower span and raised up the great bascules as the diminutive vessels passed underneath. On all the other bridges, ornamented with pylons and banners for the occasion, stood serried lines of steel-helmeted "bodyguard", and in the centre of each was a band which broke into the strains of the German national anthem as the flotilla appeared. Squadrons of bombers in formation roared up and down the river, only a few hundred feet above the heads of the crowds on the Embankment, who were allowed to peer at the spectacle through a continuous line of British police facing inwards. At Westminster Pier, where the flotilla arrived punctually as Big Ben announced noon, Hitler was met by the Cabinet, headed by Dr. Evans, who, it was afterwards stated, greeted him with the raised arm salute. It was impossible, however, for the ordinary man to see this incident, since the approaches to the pier were hedged deep with troops and a phalanx of Hitler Youth who barked out a triple "Heil!" as their Führer set foot in England.

It had originally been reported that Hitler would receive the homage of Parliament at Westminster, but this item on the programme had been abandoned, apparently because it was not yet considered politic to enforce a full attendance of both Houses, or even to reconvene that neglected organ of State. Instead, a procession of bullet-proof cars with an escort of motor-cyclist troops proceeded slowly up Whitehall towards St. James's Palace, where Hitler had elected to have his temporary residence and where a reception was to be held that afternoon. The shuttered windows of Buckingham Palace, which had witnessed so many a flashing Sovereign's escort, gazed blankly down the Mall as the new régime, surrounded by a cloud of stuttering motor-cycles, advanced towards them and then turned to the right into St. James's.

On that very day, when so much that was portentous was happening in London, the rest of the "bodyguard" set foot in England, to the number of 300,000 men. Within twenty-four hours every large port was occupied, in clockwork order, and Admiralty signals ordered all naval commanders to "co-operate" with the nearest units of the German Grand Fleet. Resistance was of the slightest, although it did leak out afterwards that some sixty British sailors and marines lost their lives at Chatham and Portsmouth.

The good news was brought to Adolf Hitler in strange surroundings. During the night he had driven westwards, through the sleeping suburbs, to fulfil a curious little ambition. At dawn, when his secretaries rushed up with the latest cables, he was the illustrious tenant of Hampton Court Palace, walking moodily among the roses wet with dew.

Chapter Six

FIXTURE AT LORD'S

AND now there were German troops stationed in London and Exeter, in York and Edinburgh and Carlisle. German words of command rang out on Salisbury Plain and in the green recesses of Ashdown Forest; steel helmets moved across the skyline of Dartmoor and the Grampian Hills. The grey Reichswehr paraded down Whitehall, deployed across Newmarket Heath, billeted itself in the stone cottages of the Cotswolds. And everywhere there went with it, like hostages, a few sullen men in khaki, who were the rightful heirs of these places, and had meant to devote their lives to defending them.

The Germans came swinging along the Mall with flowers round their bayonets, and the flowers did not wither straight away. Unprovoked, the officers remained polite, the men stonily respectful. But they smiled grimly to themselves as they proceeded to their stations, mounting their machine guns according to prearranged plan. Within three days the whole of Great Britain was effectively occupied, and the invasion was complete.

There was something apparitional about the invaders. Hitler's men—they had been so long the distant bogies whom our armed might was holding at bay, that it was unbelievable that one fine day they should arrive, as it were, by bus. You might, for instance, on Wednesday be walking down a sandy lane, to buy some cigarettes in the village, reflecting on the way how changeless was the countryside, whatever the B.B.C. might say at nine o'clock; then on Thursday, repeating the errand, you might find a company of Hessian

Jäger resting on a route march beneath the beeches, looking more or less at home in your inviolable pastures. "Ah, the Germans," you would say to yourself, rather as though they were a circus that was passing through the village. But the circus had come to stay.

Outside London, the fact that England had been seized by the enemy was brought home to many people only in flashes. Twelve months earlier most inhabitants of Debenford would have said, quite truthfully, that they would rather be dead than see German soldiers encamped on Sutton Walks. Now, by some odd conjuring trick of fortune, they were there— and Gerald Cooke wrote to us that the one complaint of the villagers was that, a well-worn short cut being now denied to them by a smiling Westphalian sentry, it was two furlongs more to Woodbridge. The parish meeting wrote to the commanding officer about this short cut, and young Captain von Krausnitz, being a clever man, at once threw it open again. Thenceforth the villagers walked through the camp with their shopping baskets, beaming with gratitude and friendliness, and fraternized to some extent with the soldiers. After all, they were hardly stranger than the actors and actresses who had turned an old sailing barge on the Deben into a weekend haunt, or worse-behaved than Londoners in their little red bungalows over the hill. Also they had money to spend. The landlord of the "Rose Revived" adapted his cellar to the keeping of lager, both *dunkles* and *helles*, on draught; the village baker learnt how to make *Milchbrödchen*. The girls began to dream of dances at Ipswich, and a few old ladies, their minds full of all the crime reports in the *Daily Mail*, were genuinely relieved that "the military", albeit grey-clad, had arrived to preserve law and order.

So wrote Gerald Cooke, from Ashdene Cottage, and to us in teeming London, now cowering under what was virtually martial law, it was a queer picture. We had indeed wanted to think of Debenford as our private refuge in this nightmare world, even if there the seasons and the crops mattered more than patriotism; but it was a shock to learn that, while we shuddered in London, the country folk were taking the enemy to their hearts.

"But", Gerald added, "there are moments when even we hang our heads. There was a bit of excitement when a picture of Hitler standing with the Chief Regent took the place of the Death of Nelson over the parlour mantelpiece at the Rose. We *almost* began to talk politics. Then you may remember that we lost five young men in the last war, two of them in the crew of a lightship. People tend to avoid their relatives.

I suggested to the Vicar that we might add the five names to the 1914 memorial, but he coughed and changed the subject. Another unhappy reminder of the wider catastrophe is the presence in the village of young Paul Ebbotson. You may remember him, son of the blacksmith, who did so well at school and got a job in the Nigerian police. Now that's all over, and he's back as a farm labourer.

"Big changes are coming, no doubt. The signs are there for those who care to read them. For some weeks now Woodbridge police court has been attended by a German officer, sitting very erect beside the mild-mannered Gestapo fellow who haunts the neighbourhood; and yesterday he was actually given a place on the bench! Stonehaven nearly had a fit, but, as the chairman seemed to take it as a matter of course, he thought it best to say nothing. The news from Ipswich is more ominous still, for it is said that the City Council is entirely under the control (lightly exercised hitherto) of the military commandant. I wonder if this is typical of England as a whole? One never reads anything of these things in the papers.

"The judge came to Ipswich last week on circuit. He had an escort of Uhlans, which wasn't very nice; in fact, there was something unpleasantly farcical about the whole business. General von So-and-So, who sat among the notabilities, must have twirled his moustaches most impatiently when all that business about *oyer* and *terminer* and our Sovereign Lord the King was being read. Very different from the People's Courts! The biggest case in the calendar, according to the *Eastern Daily News*, was a complicated civil action about an unimportant right of way. How unreal it seems to be expensively arguing a matter like this, from ancient statutes and leading cases, when the very bases of our law are crumbling!

"Never mind. No-one can chase the swallows away before their time, and I don't suppose the Germans will be pulling up the water-blobs above the mill-race. Come soon, as you both must be desperately in need of a change."

"Well," I said to Elizabeth, "shall we pay another visit to Debenford soon?"

"No," she said. "Let's wait till we know the worst. We might find it horribly changed—more than Gerald realizes, who lives there all the time. Or we might find it horribly the same, like a death mask. Let's go to some place that doesn't matter."

She pinned the enormous yellow Press badge to her dress, and went off to submit an article to the Bureau of Censorship. That week-end we went to Brighton. We didn't enjoy it at all;

and we found that even the monstrous Pavilion must have been among the things we had loved, for we were very sorry to see that it had been turned into a German barracks.

On Saturday morning we saw Jack Dorman, of the *Brisbane Star*, sitting on the beach throwing pebbles at a bottle. "Who does that stand for?" I asked. "Mr. H. or Sir J.N.?" He said, neither. It stood for the Unholy Optimists, who succeeded only in making the world seem a blacker place than ever. Asked to explain, he drew out a little notebook. "Look," he said, "I am making a collection of Unholy Optimisms—prominent people who by their statements publicly made since the arrival of German troops show that they are coldly and deliberately deceiving themselves. If the *New Statesman* hadn't been suppressed it might have published them with the title 'This Earth, this Gau, this England'."

It was indeed an extraordinary collection. Most of the people quoted are now dead—some "shot while attempting to escape"—they were none of them time-servers, and all of them, surely, must have repented of what they said. It would not be fair, therefore, to name them, but I think it should be put on record that a bishop, for instance, in Westminster Abbey described Hitler as "the Reformation ideal of a Christian prince", and that the proprietor of a great newspaper remarked "How fortunate and right it is that the Führer admires the English character!" It was a progressive member of the New English Art Club who said, "National Socialism is the disciplined renascence of wonder," and a famous headmaster who assured parents that Hitler's *Ordenburgen* were but a flattering translation into a German idiom of the English public school. There was *Nordic Iron*, the fatuous poem done in the manner, but not with the intent, of *The Waste Land*, and there was the elder statesman's advice to "show the Germans something worth imitating". A song sung by a top-of-the-bill comedian had a chorus which went "Belinda is now quite the Belle of Berlin, and Lotte's the Lily of London"; and the public orator at a university which was admitting Goebbels to an honorary degree addressed him with the words *"Egregie doctor, mores instrue, et nostra tecum pectora in Valhallam trahe"*.

All this was perpetrated while German troops, at vantage points throughout the three kingdoms, were quietly but relentlessly preparing to press down the heel. It was perpetrated by men who were trapped, but were too vain to know it—who would never believe that the values they had made their own could be entirely falsified by brute force, and preferred to persuade themselves that God and the snail were still somehow where they ought to be. They were not cowards but fools.

All three of us picked up the largest stone we could find, and hurled it at the bottle. It splintered into fragments. A Prussian bugle call sounded from the Royal Pavilion. Though no-one in Brighton knew it, it was ushering in *Der Tag*, the twenty-four hours in which the heel was actually to be pressed down, in good earnest.

. . . Far away in Whitechapel there was one, Isaac Cohen, who was no Unholy Optimist. He made no attempt to deceive himself, and he foresaw, as clearly as though it had already begun to happen, what was in store for his race, his class, and, ultimately, his adopted country. Millions of others foresaw all this too, and many of his race, following the despairing example of their brethren in all the desecrated capitals, from Paris to Vienna, put an end to themselves and their families. Others shut their eyes and ears and tried to forget. Isaac Cohen did neither of these things. He dwelt on the future, by night as well as by day, until his ears rang with the cries of future martyrs and he saw the desolation of a yet uncreated ghetto. As with a drunkard, his mental vision contracted as it sharpened; he saw the Terror with frightful clarity, but round it there was mist and vagueness. Only out of this darkness loomed the shadowy figure of a man, with little pig's eyes, and a small moustache, and a lock of lank hair plastered to his forehead. This figure, vague as it was, was yet essential to terrible sharp vision in the centre. Every night Isaac Cohen became more certain that one had to remove the figure for the vision to soften, lose definition, and, at last, break down and disappear. Only destroy the figure . . .

One day, in a Lyons shop on the Mile End Road, Isaac Cohen fell into conversation with a Gentile, a German who confessed to being a Social Democrat. He was a sympathetic fellow, this German, and it was not long before Isaac Cohen was staggering out his nightmare into friendly ears. There was much earnest conversation between the two, the one man whispering wildly, the other calming him, directing his thoughts, narrowing his vision once again. A shiny black object changed hands before the interview was over.

There was no sleep for Isaac Cohen the next three nights. His brain was racing; no longer was the evil figure haunting the periphery of his mind, it was gaining definition, moving into the centre, marching boldly up to a dais in the midst of an applauding multitude. And it became thinner and thinner until it was like a thread—the thread upon which alone that other fearful vision depended. . . .

When the bugle sounded we stopped the silly game of throwing stones, and climbed back on to the promenade. I bought an evening paper. "Hell!" I said. "Mr. H. has decided to attend that youth parade in London to-morrow morning, and he may make a speech. Dorman, you and I will have to go back. Another week-end ruined!"

One could not ignore Hitler's speeches. He made them seldom, and when he did we hung on his words and lost no opportunity, within the strict limits of the censorship, of "interpreting" them. Sometimes we might add: "The Prime Minister also spoke".

But at the seaside, even in the vulgar pullulation of Brighton, the Führer seemed somehow remote. Politics never had much to do with groins and pebbles and seaweed, and the sun glared too fiercely on the *Evening Standard* for it to be read with comfort. We picked our way along an inert line of deck-chairs, and wondered at those comfortable people whose lives were still sufficiently shored up by giltedged securities or sheltered jobs that they could gaze placidly into the blue. They were Canutes who did not even notice the sea.

But for the chance that Hitler would speak at it I should have been glad to give the Young Englander parade a miss. It takes time to get inured to the rites of Moloch, and I preferred the disbanded Boy Scouts. Moreover, I had no desire to be present at the desecration of Lord's cricket ground. I felt deeply for the head groundsman, who a week before had walked away and had never been heard of since.

Next morning was fresh and sunlit—just the morning, had it been a Saturday, for the opening day of Middlesex *v.* Surrey. But the scene was cruelly different. The sacred pavilion was full of strange uniforms, and the ring of spectators was glum and silent. A brass band played discordantly. Only the turf remained inviolate; but round it were ranged, ready for marching, the grim imported Hitler Youth, and our own poor lads, in their new jackboots and white peaked caps. Their horrible banners, red and black, moved in the gentle breeze.

Dorman and I gazed miserably at the green island, so soon to be submerged. It was poignantly symbolic. For a moment the ghosts, Francis Thompson's, appeared, and the run-stealers flickered to and fro. But then the music crashed out, and two flesh-and-blood figures moved into that holy place. One was that poor, aged Duke of Mercia who somehow had consented to be made Lord President of the Council and Chief Regent, representative of the vacant Throne. I recalled, with a slight shock, that not many years ago he had been proud to be President of the M.C.C. Perhaps his old eyes did not see what we saw, and he thought he was strolling about at lunch-time during the Eton and Harrow match. But now beside him stalked Herr Hitler.

Two figures, then, alone in that great green expanse. No, there were three, for a little dark man appeared out of the crowd, running, gesticulating, shouting. Hitler stood still; the old Duke stumbled on into his dreams. The man was waving something, it was a gun. He fired twice, and Adolf Hitler rolled heavily on to the turf.

In the next few minutes was concentrated the first stunning impact of the long-delayed blow which put an end to the liberties and happiness of England. It was an execution, carried out with swiftness, precision and a certain solemnity.

The Black Guards behind Hitler shot the assailant dead. A large force of Brown Shirts appeared from nowhere, and formed a square round the pitch, facing the spectators with levelled revolvers. Reichswehr men occupied the pavilion, where machine guns were seen trained from the scoring box. A bevy of nurses fluttered over the Führer's inert body, and bore it off to a waiting ambulance. The leader of the Hitler Youth stepped in front of the young aristocrat who was supposed to be commanding the Young Englanders, and briskly ordered them to march off the field. Messengers sped to and fro, as though on appointed errands.

I watched in dumb amazement. It was like being at the Aldershot Tattoo, except that it was disconcerting to be looking down the barrel of a Brownshirt's revolver. We were all standing up, but a peremptory voice told us to sit down again. Göring was at the microphone, and for a silly moment I likened him to a headmaster who was at last about to punish the whole school. Then I reflected that he had been named as Hitler's successor.

His guttural English throbbed across the arena as the loudspeakers, pointing different ways, caught up the words, "A terrible outrage has been committed," they boomed. "A cowardly attempt has been made on the life of our Führer. We cannot tell yet whether he has been mortally wounded. The crime must be avenged. The German nation assumes this duty. The necessary measures will be taken."

Is it true that the Field-Marshal glanced at a piece of paper in his hand to make sure that he got his English sentences right? I was too scared to notice. At any rate, it would only have been the last touch of absurdity in this gigantic and hideous charade.

The band struck up something like a dead march, and the German occupants of the tribune began to move out across the green space, empty now except for the huddled body of Isaac Cohen. The British notabilities hesitated, and at length, led by the Prime Minister, retired into the interior of the pavilion. Goebbels, as he passed, savagely kicked the corpse of the Jew. The Duke was left alone. Sublime in his grey top-hat, he stumbled off in the wrong direction, and was hustled out at the Nursery End by a party of Stormtroopers. The band played "Deutschland über Alles" and the "Horst Wessel Lied", and omitted to play "God Save the King".

"Keep your seats." It was Himmler now at the microphone. "No-one may leave before examination by the authorities." The Hitler Youth, without the least hesitation, assumed the task of shepherding the great crowd, one by one, through only four exits, where each individual was questioned at length by a Gestapo man. The news soon spread that there was a fleet of black marias outside to take those the Nazis disliked to gaol.

A good quarter of Britain's well-known figures were present on the ground—trapped. Judges, bishops, generals—for all we knew the prisons were ready to snap up any of them. It was very different from that party at Bush House, with its champagne and Wagner. The sun beat down, and, rank on rank, the people sat nearly motionless, waiting to be marshalled to the exits by fourteen-year-old boys.

No special consideration was shown to the Press. We wanted to rush off and telephone our stories, but Dr. Schultz appeared and distributed a typewritten statement which announced that no messages for oversea would be accepted that day beyond the official communiqué which had already been transmitted.

What was in that communiqué? We were not told. We did not even know whether Hitler was dead. We did not know whether to wish he were. We could only guess at what was happening outside in London, our London, beyond the tall houses of St. John's Wood.

There was no panic. That is to say, people did not brave the machine guns and make a rush to the turnstiles. They waited, and either wept or sat quite motionless.

After a while the microphones announced that the Führer, by the intervention of Providence, had not been killed but only wounded in the arm. A sibilant murmur came up from the crowd. I suppose they were muttering to each other "A frame-up", and then telling each other "Hush!" I thought at once of Elmer Rice's *Judgement Day*.

I saw my old friend von Holtz, breathing rather heavily, with set face. I could not resist a feeble jest. "Surely, *this* is the most notable event of the London season," I said; but he looked away without answering.

They were a long time coming to the row on which I was sitting. It was blazing noon, and one felt slightly sick, and the grass looked so green with, in the middle of it, the one dark crumpled figure that no-one seemed to clear away. For a moment I dropped off to sleep, and woke expecting to hear the click of the ball on the bat and a polite murmur of "Well played, sir."

Dorman, who was sitting beside me, was calmly surveying the scene with a pair of field-glasses. He turned them here and there, sweeping across the sea of unhappy faces, until they lighted upon the crumpled solitary object in the middle of the field. "Looks like a Jew," he muttered, and then he turned to me. "You know, Fenton," he said, somewhat excitedly, "when they publish the name and circumstances of that poor wretch I'm going to do a little detective work on my own. I should like to know how he got hold of that revolver in these days—and whether he was the sort of man who could distinguish live cartridges from blank ones." "Shut up, you fool," I whispered. "You can't play Lord Peter Wimsey here." I glanced round. There, behind us, sat the comfortable Dr. Schultz, blinking through his spectacles like a West Country rector at the Oxford and Cambridge match. He made no sign.

"Row C 16, please." It was our turn. Two hours after the process had begun there must still have been three-fourths of the crowd left waiting. Sixteen of us trooped meekly to the designated exit I bade farewell to Dorman.

"Charles Arthur Fenton," repeated the Gestapo man seated at the table, and in a moment an underling had turned up my name in an enormous book. "*So!* Correspondent of the *Wellington Courier*. Messages unfriendly in tone. Contacts with the late Stephen Mallory. Well, Mr. Fenton, I don't think I need detain you—now; but you know how to be careful, don't you?"

He handed me a thing like a disembarkation card, which I surrendered to an S.S. man at the gate. I drew a deep breath when I got outside; and then I realized that this was foolish, for I was not walking into the freedom I had known.

A special single-sheet edition of the Sunday papers confirmed my worst fears. An official statement said that, owing to the increasing anarchy in Great Britain, which had culminated in a dastardly attempt on the Führer's life, the German Government had been obliged to take temporary control of the country. The Evans Ministry was suspended from office and a state of emergency amounting to martial law was proclaimed. For greater security 200,000 more German troops and police had landed at East Coast ports. Certain arrests had been made.

I knew that the Terror had come.

Chapter Seven

TERROR

ELIZABETH and I spent that evening in miserable silence in our Hampstead flat. Conversation, we found, was only a sharing of terrifying conjectures, and though we both made a pretence of reading we found that we could neither of us keep our minds on our books. There was no going out, for the authorities had imposed a curfew at eight o'clock with a warning that anyone found out in the streets after that hour would run the risk of being shot without trial as a disturber of public order. There was little traffic for the same reason, but occasionally a high-powered car roared by up the High Street, and once, hearing the noise of motor-cycles, I looked out and saw a lorry with a party of men huddled on it and an escort of motorized troops going northwards. The late news on the wireless announced that the Germans had taken over the whole administrative machinery of the country and had occupied every fortress, warship, dock, and public building. We neither of us felt any surprise; any smaller achievement would have been unworthy of Hitler's record of efficient crime. Our main concern was with a question not touched on by the wireless and one that everyone must have been asking that night. Had there been, were there going to be, many arrests?

"It would be so unnecessary," said Elizabeth. "He's got us all where he wants us, and now's his time to become a comparatively mild and likeable tyrant."

"Impossible!" I said. "He hasn't got it in him. Revenge is

sweet, and anyhow he can't afford to take risks, as the case of poor Mallory shows. Didn't I tell you about all those black marias outside Lord's? Why, he might have taken the Archbishop of Canterbury for a ride in one of them, for all we know."

I described my interview with the fellow at the turnstile, and we agreed that I must have got ticket-of-leave while on good behaviour. We discussed the chances of my being able to cable worth-while messages again, and wondered whether my paper, in despair, would summon us back to Wellington. "Let's see what Dorman thinks about it," I said, and picked up the telephone. But after I had dialled the number I heard only the operator's voice repeating flatly what she must have said over and over again that evening: "Sorry, but no private calls are allowed this evening. We hope to have the regular service established again by to-morrow."

So even the telephones were to come under surveillance. We sat digesting the implications of this new evidence of our helplessness when suddenly I heard the approaching roar of one of the police cars coming up the hill again. But this time it stopped, and looking out of the window in the late summer dusk I saw that it had halted immediately outside our block of flats. I turned to warn Elizabeth, but she was beside me. "No!" she said in a breaking voice, "it can't be you they want." We stood in breathless silence listening. In that silence the ring of the bell in the flat below sounded almost as loud as our own. We heard the door open, and then a muffled sound of raised voices and a trampling of feet. I went out of our flat and tip-toed to the stair-head, whence I could see on to the lower landing. I could hear both a man's and a woman's voice raised in expostulation. They were cut short by a sharp order in a guttural voice. There was the horrid sound of blows, a piercing shriek from the woman, and a deep groan. Then the stalwart form of a Brownshirt appeared backing out of the front door. He and another were carrying out the body of our neighbour, Harry Wolffman, a spruce Jew in the clothing trade, whom I had met often enough on the stairs. For one moment the light on the landing fell on the unconscious upturned face with a streak of blood across the forehead, and then they had stumbled down the staircase with their burden. For a moment longer I heard the heartbroken sobbing of his wife, and then a German officer left the flat, slamming the door behind him. I drew back, feeling a coward as I did so, lest he should look up and see me. I went back to the flat, finding that I had left the door open, and that inside Elizabeth lay with her face buried in the cushions of the couch. But she recovered from the horror quicker than I, and went down to see what she could do for Mrs. Wolffman. Presently she brought up a sobbing, shivering woman who could do little but cry "Why do they take him? What has my Harry done? He is so kind a man, he wouldn't hurt a fly. He refuse to give money to the Greyshirts, yes. But that was business. Never would he plot against their Hitler." Elizabeth soothed her at last, gave her a sleeping draught, and put her in the spare room.

We looked out from our window on to the panorama of a darkling London. Lights twinkled everywhere; it might have been the gay city of before the war. "My God," I said, "if they're coming after the small fry like this, what can't be happening down there?" Then we drew the curtains and tried to get some sleep.

The next morning I was called from my bed by the telephone. A crisp German military voice spoke. "Mr. Fenton of the newspaper *Vellington Courier*? You haf a frent Jack Dorman, of the newspaper *Brisbane Star*, no? This Dorman is in arrest of vords against the Führer hafing sboken. He gif your name to sbeak for him. You vill to the State Emergency Court at Voodside Bark report, blease." When I had recovered my breath I asked at what time I should report, and was told that a police car would fetch me that morning. I must be ready for its arrival.

I broke the news to Elizabeth, and, though we were both scared, neither of us could believe that Jack Dorman had said anything to implicate me. Although his messages to his paper had been, I knew, models of discretion, he had spoken his mind in privacy with a wholly Australian pungency. He belonged to the "tough" school of correspondent, and was not prone to mince his words. I told Elizabeth that if they had been going to arrest me they would not have given me any warning, instancing the fate of poor Harry Wolffman, whose wife still kept to her room this morning. Elizabeth pretended to be reassured, and I to be calm, but we neither of us liked to look at the other.

The police car arrived soon after breakfast. A smart young Brownshirt saluted me with "Heil Hitler" to which I meekly replied, and escorted me down to the car. I climbed into the back; the Brownshirt got in beside the driver and we set off. Beside me in the back sat another civilian. He was white and silent, and we neither of us exchanged any conversation.

At Woodside Park was situated the huge private mental home which the German police had inspected soon after their arrival. A sentry was posted at the gate, and stopped the car on our arrival. After a word from our Brownshirt, we were admitted into the grounds, and deposited at the front door of the huge brick edifice. I was taken straightway down an echoing corridor patrolled by more sentries, and shown into a small and comfortless waiting-room. There, I was told, I must sit until someone came to conduct me to the tribunal. There was no sign of my late companion in the car. He had been taken in charge by two armed guards, and I judged that his case was worse than mine. There was an extraordinary silence in the little room. Outside I could hear the tread of the sentries and the sound of distant voices. Once I heard, or thought I heard, a muffled cry, but a door slammed and there was silence. I looked out of the window into the neglected grounds. There was nothing to be seen but a pile of newly turned clay in a far corner of one of the lawns.

After a long time—it was only about an hour really, I suppose—the door opened and the same young Brownshirt appeared. "Please to come," he said abruptly. I followed him down the passage, and up a staircase, into a long room with windows down the side. It might once have been a ward; now a few benches and a long table at one end had turned it into a court. I was told to take my seat on one of the benches. Behind the table sat three men in the black uniform of the S.S.; two were middle-aged and were consulting papers, the third was a youth of not more than twenty-two with fair curly hair and blue eyes. He was leaning back idly flicking the polished side of his boot with a riding crop and appeared supremely bored with the whole proceedings. He favoured me with a brief stare when I came in, and resumed his lounging attitude, whistling softly "Du schöne Violetta".

Then the door behind me opened again and into the room was half-pushed and half-carried what was left of Jack Dorman. His clothes were torn and dusty and he was dragging one leg as if it was broken. When one of his guards seized him roughly by the shoulder he winced and shuddered as if his whole body was sore. But when he saw me, his white face broke into some semblance of its old devil-may-care smile. "Good of you to come, Fenton," he said hoarsely. "Sorry to drag you all this way." "Silence," shouted one of the middle-aged judges, and a guard struck him over the mouth.

The proceedings were mostly in German, and consisted mainly of one of the judges muttering over the contents of a typewritten document to the others. Dorman was kept upright between his guards before the table. I was conscious of feeling alternately burning hot and deadly cold as I contemplated his agony and my helplessness. Suddenly my name was called and I stood up. The young man addressed me in a drawling Oxford accent almost too perfect to be believed.

"Mr. Fenton, I am Captain Hasslacher. These are my colleagues on the State Emergency Court. Will you please tell us what you know of this man?"

I said that to my knowledge he was a good and careful correspondent of an important Australian newspaper. Captain Hasslacher smiled. "The *Brisbane Star* an important paper? Come, Mr. Fenton, we must not exaggerate, or we may be considered a partial witness. That would be most unfortunate for us and for the defendant. What do you know of his private life?"

I said that I knew he was a bachelor, living alone, and that as far as I was concerned his honesty and reputation were above reproach.

"But his conversation, Mr. Fenton. Just a little—shall we say, rash, was it not?"

Mr. Dorman, I said, was an Australian and as such was inclined to use rather more forcible expressions than were customary in this country. I was quite sure that these were no more than the idiom of his nation, and had no undue political significance. Captain Hasslacher raised his fair eyebrows and pursed his lips. "I'm afraid we have information that some of the expressions he has used about prominent personages are *quite* inexcusable," he said playfully. I could only repeat that they had not been used in my presence, and that from my knowledge of Dorman's character I did not think he was likely to have used them. Captain Hasslacher laughed. "I'm afraid you are inclined to be partial after all, Mr. Fenton," he said and turned to his colleagues. There was a brief conference and then the central figure addressed Dorman sternly in German. When he had concluded Captain Hasslacher said: "He explains, Mr. Dorman, that your vocabulary will be improved by a brief stay in our brand-new holiday camp at Godalming. You will meet such nice people there. That is all." He sat down with a charming smile, and I think I have never hated any man more.

Dorman was hustled out. I caught a muffled "Thanks" as he passed me, but he was obviously dizzy with pain or lack of sleep and looked likely to faint at any minute. Then my Brownshirt friend touched me on the shoulder and I was escorted out of the building, down the drive and into what seemed the comparative freedom and sanity of a deserted suburban road.

I stumbled blindly on into a world of errand boys and

perambulators, past an old lady dropping a letter into a red pillar-box marked "G.R.", and into a little L.C.C. park where children were playing. I slumped heavily down upon a seat, opposite the railed-in pond. A boy, hands in pockets, went whistling by. The sun shone on the water. "From troubles of the world I turn to ducks."

Elizabeth would be waiting. Heavens, I must ring her up. No, of course, the telephones were not available. I ran out of the park gates, down a tree-shaded street, until I came to shops and tramlines. I wanted a taxi, but there was none in sight. I caught a bus. It was the wrong one. Altogether, it took me three-quarters of an hour to get home.

In battle, though it be in a smiling countryside, there is drawn somewhere that invisible line, so vividly described in *War and Peace*, which separates the known world of camps and comradeship from unknown sufferings and death. Now such a line cut across these commonplace London streets, with their butchers' shops and knots of women shoppers—a line beyond which lay the way to those echoing corridors down which Jack Dorman had been dragged. Before long every man, woman and child of those everyday crowds would be conscious of it, night and day.

When I did reach home I told Elizabeth of my experiences and of my belief that Dorman's rash remark at Lord's had got him into this trouble.

"You see," I said to Elizabeth, "they can't let a man like that loose. This story of Hitler's being wounded in the arm is transparent enough, but it would never do to have it demolished completely with any actual evidence."

"Then why haven't they just deported him?"

"I suppose it is that he has made some enemies with his tongue, and they are taking advantage of the situation."

"Oh, Charles darling, what enemies have *you* made?"

I laughed, but not very convincingly. "I have been very very discreet," I said, as my mind raced back over all my indiscretions.

Then the telephone bell rang. Elizabeth picked up the receiver before I could grasp it. She turned still paler. "No, no," she said quickly, "I don't think he's in."

"It's Dr. Schultz," she said, with her hand over the mouth-piece. "Oh, they'll take you. I know they will."

"I'd better speak to him," I said, and took the receiver from her.

But Dr. Schultz's tones were kindly. "So you are at home, Mr. Fenton," he said. "How fortunate. I give you the ring to assure you that correspondents can once again by cable send their messages. Now, a suggestion please. Your friend, Mr. Dorman, I worry about him. I think he will not like the climate of Godalming. So fine a man, he should be released, you don't think?"

"Yes, yes," I cried, and launched into a passionate plea for my friend. Dr. Schultz interrupted me.

"But we are agreed. Together we may succeed in his release, and immediate departure for his native land. We must let the truth be known. You were present at his trial. So fair, was it not?"

"It was nothing of the sort," I said. "My dear Dr. Schultz, you would have been disgusted if you had been there. It was a sheer farce, and——"

"As you say, Mr. Fenton, it was a fair trial. A fact, no doubt, of some interest to the Antipodes. You must tell your readers, Mr. Fenton, and—don't you say?—'Australian papers please to copy.' Then, no doubt, Mr. Dorman will repay your efforts with a like discretion. You too, I think, would feel less happy at Godalming. I expect you, perhaps, at the Bureau in one hour."

He rang off. He had made himself quite clear.

If you have lived in London under the Captivity, if you have seen a friend after the Gestapo have had him, if you yourself have been threatened with the concentration camp and have had to reach such a decision as mine in the presence of your wife—then you have a right to judge me. I did what Dr. Schultz asked. Next morning's issue of the *Wellington Courier* carried a fuller story of the political changes in England than any other paper abroad, and one which, by special arrangement, was afterwards reproduced pretty extensively in Australia and the United States. It was accurate, if strictly censored, but in the middle of it appeared a curious paragraph, sharing with the rest the full authority of "Our Own Correspondent". It read:

"Among some persons who appeared on political charges before the Emergency Courts was Mr. Jack Dorman, the London Correspondent of the *Brisbane Star*. I myself was invited to give evidence of character on his behalf, upon which the Court made no attempt to examine the case against the accused, which presumably had been brought by some false denouncer. Mr. Dorman was released the same day."

This was a good stroke of German propaganda. The censor left nothing else in my message on the subject of arrests and imprisonments, so that it gave an impression almost exactly contrary to the truth. Thus a day or two passed before the outside world came to believe the worst. It took the usurpers about that time to climb firmly enough into the saddle to be able to throw away the mask. But I am not really sorry I did it.

Dr. Schultz winked at me. "Very creditable, Mr. Fenton, very creditable," he said, when he had seen my paragraph. "You understand us Germans so well. What a shame you cannot put down your services at the dispositions of Reichs-minister Dr. Goebbels." He was just the same old Schultz, sitting back in his padded chair, even though his genial empire now rested openly on torture and blood. The incongruity was terrifying.

The authentic facts about the Terror are by this time too well known; it is hardly necessary any longer for the Germans to conceal them. I myself added my testimony when I got back to New Zealand, in a series of articles which regard for historical truth compelled me to write, but which, I think, made wearisome as well as sickening reading.

Searches and arrests went on steadily for three days. As civilized life contracted and the streets were emptied of ordinary passers-by it was almost as though one could constantly hear, from this quarter and that, the sound of splintered wood, the cries of men and the screams of women. Perhaps this was an illusion of the nerves, but the records show that at every hour of the day and night the raids and arrests continued.

The card-indexes snapped in and out at Bush House. No doubt von Holtz's came in useful, in a negative sense. By about the middle of the week more than 10,000 people had been apprehended.

Lists were published from time to time. One glanced anxiously down the long strings of names, surprised that the Nazis had been waiting to pounce all this time on so many obscure people, in Leicester or Wolverhampton, that one had never heard of before. Then some household name would leap to the eye—a Jewish scientist, a famous headmaster, a liberal-minded dean. Little by little, it was clear, the effective voice of Britain was being silenced.

The fearless opponents of Hitlerism went first—those who had never wavered in their condemnation of the Nazi evil, on higher grounds than those of patriotism. They were followed by others of the brave and the true, who had trod the simple path of duty until it had been lost in the post-Nuremberg morass. But the cowards were taken too, if being at liberty they might be an embarrassment to the conquerors; and not even the most flagrant compromisers escaped. In vain had certain mayors exhausted the borough treasury in entertaining the Nazi commandant, or civil servants thrown open official secrets to their German "advisers". *Proditores, etiam iis quos anteponunt, invisi sunt.* The Nazis had plenty of fun later with people as contemptible as themselves.

Not all, of course, of the former leaders of the nation, whether admirals or street orators, could be accommodated in the centres of "protective custody". But all could be threatened with such a fate, and made to dance a tune that would ward it off. The Führer's Government must be carried on, and it could not be done entirely by foreign policemen. I do not for one moment blame those who now accepted minor office under the Nazis. I do not blame them for saluting the Swastika flag, or even for taking an enforced oath of loyalty to Adolf Hitler. A sanitary inspector, after all, has as great a responsibility to a conquered as to a free people. The essential betrayal had happened long before, and a man, it is said, must eat. Nevertheless, there were some who faced privation rather than submit, or preferred even suicide to the life the Nazis offered them.

Most of those destined for concentration camps were hurried away on the authority of some minor functionary of the Gestapo; "trials", such as that undergone by Dorman, were arranged only for special purposes. But the chosen personifications of the spirit that had once flouted Hitler's will—men like Churchill, Duff Cooper and Eden—were seized upon with a special savagery that demanded a certain formal satisfaction. The horror of the proceedings in Westminster Hall, when these men were made to answer charges that suggested they were the enemies of civilization itself, is well enough known through the official descriptions. But those descriptions, shouted into the microphone by excited Nazi announcers, failed to make one point clear—they never admitted how far the Public Prosecutor was from shaking the proud resignation of the victims.

As for the members of the deposed Evans Government, they were under house arrest at Chequers. There they lived in luxury, walking beneath the summer trees and playing billiards. "Tiny pleasures occupied the place of glories and of duties." It was very cruel, and one was almost sorry for them.

So, in a few short days, the great superstructure of English life was hacked down, but too much else was happening for us to notice how complete the destruction was. For the Germans there was manly work to be done—the sort of thing that got one the Iron Cross. It was not only to be a question of torturing people in the new concentration camps; there was to be a certain amount of standing people against a wall to be shot.

First there were the remnants of the British army, navy, and air force to be disarmed and demobilized. The quickest way to do this, if ever the slightest resistance was shown, was to take the men by surprise and mow them down with machine guns. This resulted in about 3,000 deaths, chiefly at Chatham and Aldershot, and thirteen Iron Crosses.

Another problem was that of giving adequate security to thouse who went about their Führer's business. A sergeant of the Gestapo, for instance, was actually shot at Chester-le-Street by the enraged father of a young girl, and at Peterborough a German officer who struck an old man for alleged insolence was thrown by the crowd into the Nene. It was found difficult to bring these crimes home to their real perpetrator, so certain quarters of Chester-le-Street and Peterborough were decimated, one strong healthy man, preferably a father of a family, being taken from every three or four houses. Throughout the country about 4,500 people perished in this way.

The German refugees (thouse which even the Evans Government had avoided sending back to Germany) were dealt with by a simple plan. If there was no information required from them by the Gestapo all that happened was that a party of Brownshirts visited their homes and shot them. There was, however, a slight disadvantage in this procedure, as it led to various people being killed by mistake.

But not all the refugees were treated in quite this way. I well remember how worried we were about Mr. and Mrs. Essener, another German couple in our block of flats, living just above us. They were very attractive and pathetic people, not Jews, but professed enemies of the Nazis, and they used to tell us some horrible stories about their sufferings before they escaped. "They're for it any time now," I told Elizabeth. Then one evening she ran in to say that she had caught sight of a man in a Brownshirt's uniform entering their flat. We waited breathlessly on the landing. Within two minutes the door was reopened, and through the bannisters we could see the Brownshirt's feet and also those of a woman. So Essener was out, and it was his pretty wife that this swine was taking away. Elizabeth drew me back into the doorway, fearing I might do something foolish, and in a moment the couple, descending the stairs, passed across our field of vision. The Brownshirt turned towards us; a smile of recognition lit up his features; and he shot out his hand with a genial "Heil Hitler!" It was our old friend Herr Essener, late a "refugee", taking his wife out for a walk on the Heath.

Then there were our own Jews—not the rich ones, who for the most part had escaped long ago, but the hard-working professional men and the huddled families of Whitechapel, Leeds, and Cheetham Hill, Manchester. The former, whatever their calling, faced the progressive disasters of a *numerus clausus*, a general boycott, and then an uncompromising "Aryan clause" which meant penury and sometimes starvation. The latter, now at the mercy of all that was meanest and most cowardly in our diseased national life, cowered hopelessly in their slums.

There is no doubt that the Germans had assigned to the Greyshirts the dirtiest work of all in the process of Nazifying Britain. It costs nothing, after supper, to throw a dog a bone, and the Greyshirts, who were to be the only vocal section of the English public, and were expected to absorb a high proportion of it, were to be thrown the bone of violent anti-Semitism. The Nazi conquerors had attained to a certain refinement of sadism, and in Great Britain they had more interesting quarry than the Jews; but for the right kind of native the cutting of the rabbis' beards and the gutting of synagogues ought to provide an acceptable consolation prize. It was the art of government, as Hitler saw it.

But I must hasten to say that the Greyshirts now were not quite those passionate crusaders that at Leeds had shown there was "blood in Britain" and had gone blindly on to produce that anarchy which had brought the enemy within the gates. Nor were they those smart paraders that had achieved such an inappropriate respectability as soon as the first of the German police arrived. Herr Meyer had got to work, and he chose his men carefully. While Rosse pirouetted in the polite world, or what remained of it, Meyer was quietly making changes in the personnel. The Grey Army that resulted had lost its spontaneous flair, but gained in brutal purpose. It was staffed by ex-convicts, not by fanatics, and it was much more efficient.

The day came when Patrick Rosse was invited to take high office in the new slave-State—in fact, to become Chief Slave. On the same day he was presented with his reorganized Greyshirts, as a new and more effective instrument of tyranny. It was then, so far as the facts are known, that he came to his senses. Precisely how he reacted I cannot say, though I have often tried to guess. The world he had lived and fought in had always been unreal, but now self-deception was no longer possible, and he was face to face with a very ugly reality.

He was, after all, no conscious Quisling, and he disappeared abruptly from the political scene. The new Leader of the Greyshirts was a fat man called Jones, who possessed a criminal record, was a sexual pervert, and had been a Communist before the collapse of the Stalin régime.

I have described, in the articles of which I speak, something of the horrors of the concentration camps, as told me by people who went through them and somehow came out alive. For the great and the good the worst tortures were reserved, but perhaps they had spiritual resources which enabled them best to withstand them. I only know that we who remained outside, whatever our circumstances might be, seemed to live always in the shadow of those cruelties. Sound in wind and limb, digging in our own garden, perhaps, or enjoying a good cigar after dinner, we could never forget that on this same island there were thousands of innocent people—very fine people, some of them—to whom life was all darkness and pain.

Godalming, among the Surrey hills, was the largest camp, and had perhaps the most distinguished register of guests. At one time it held seven judges, two Anglican and four Catholic bishops, and many more than a quorum of the old House of Commons. Himmler used to remark dreamily that it was in very lovely country. Nearly as important was the establishment at Haworth (Hitler, it seems, had once read a translation of *Jane Eyre*), where the landscape was different but the sufferings were the same. There was also a camp at Watersmeet, so that Brendon Water sometimes ran with blood, and there were others among the Scottish heather and the proud valleys of South Wales. But the most dreaded of all was the camp at Stoke Poges, within a stone's throw of the elegiac churchyard; its commandant was, I think, insane. I shall never forget the frantic plea of a Reader in Classics at London University, on being told that he would be held in "protective custody" there. "Stoke Poges!" he screamed. "No, no, not Stoke Poges! Anywhere but Stoke Poges! Please don't send me to Stoke Poges!" Was there ever a transfer of associations so cruelly ironic?

The sword of Damocles hung over everybody's head. It hung over mine, but I did not regard the risk as serious. True, I was out of favour with the authorities, but I was hardly an object of their vengeance, and, apart from Dorman, no representative of the foreign Press had been molested. Still, I tried to persuade Elizabeth to go back to New Zealand, taking Julia with her, but she would not hear of it. I fancy she thought that if she stayed she might restrain me from running into trouble. But, believe me, no-one could have taken greater care about that than I did.

I have even to confess that in the midst of all these horrors I spent an evening at the Nibelungs Club. I hated the place—more, now, of course, than ever. A sense of mere decency, you may say, should have led me to avoid even passing its doors. But put it this way. I was a journalist, whose duty it was to keep contacts bright with those who mattered. The Nibelungs Club, I imagined, being the really top-drawer expression of Anglo-Germanism, was now a very important centre indeed. Moreover, to be seen there, I thought, would be enough to wipe out any disfavour I had fallen into with the authorities, and so perhaps lead the censors to deal with me more kindly. Therefore, when "Odin", one of the few surviving gossip-writers in London, invited me to join him there for a brandy after dinner, I was rather pleased to go.

But, as I say, I hated the place. There was something about its atmosphere which suggested a ruddy apple rotten at the core. It made me think of Nietzsche in evening dress, of political religiosity pursued in a boudoir, of the athleticism of Captain Röhm. It had been founded shortly after Nuremberg by a group of cadets of notable English families who had found, in an uncertain world, one very easy way to the illusion of self-respect—the flattering attentions of their kind, *hochgeboren* also, in the Nazi ranks. Young men and women who owed their high privileges to an English past, and yet wished to feel that they were on the crest of the wave that was thundering on towards a German future, there learnt the art of being feudal and Fascist at the same time. They worked hard in the gymnasium, but drank rather too much; they read Spengler and Rosenberg, but produced a pseudo-Byronic literature of their own; they talked much of awaking the British worker to a new sense of his dignity, but they loved it when blood flowed in the East End.

The women were strange. Some were intense and earnest, simply dressed, with a perverse kind of appeal; they were in love with Hitler, or Ribbentrop, or (unconfessedly) with Patrick Rosse. Others did not dispense with the more customary feminine charms, which they freely exerted upon the Nazi visitors as they swept through the well-appointed rooms in clothes which, as one might have said in the old days, would have kept a German workman's family for years.

But the men, I thought, were all contemptible. They were time-servers and petty bullies, without wit, perseverance, or courage, and the lack of moral stamina which brought them to such a place revealed itself in all they said and did. Yet, as the German influence in England grew, there were plenty who thought that to be on good terms with the Honourable Graham Medlincote, Lord John St. Neots, or Mr. Peter de Courcy was to have a friend at court.

I had expected on this occasion to find the rooms swarming with Germans, but there was hardly one to be seen. "Strange," mused "Odin", "I hope the counts and barons are not at some function elsewhere that I ought to have known about."

The company had certainly lost much of their accustomed assurance. As I remembered them, they had been given to much decorous back-slapping, as being all superior Naziphils together. They would stand looking down through the plate-glass on the still unregenerate crowds, throw out their pigeon chests, and wink knowingly at some brownshirted princeling, or even at the assiduous von Holtz, as though to say, "We have a great task in front of us." Now they tended to turn aside from that window when a Black Guard patrol went by, and drifted into the library to read the *Tatler*.

The change was startling. It certainly seemed to worry "Odin", who began to hint that we might finish the evening elsewhere. But by this time Mr. Medlincote and Lord John had joined us, and were much more their old selves. The cause of their revival was, to be frank, champagne.

As a matter of fact, everyone now seemed to be drinking rather heavily. There was nothing much else to do. After some time a girl with short hair began discussing in a loud voice the merits of three distinct techniques for liquidating non-Aryans, as described to her by Himmler; and a still more odious woman quoted with relish certain private witticisms of the Führer made at the expense of British personalities now in concentration camps.

Medlincote leant his flushed face towards me. "My dear boy," he said, "d'you know where we are? Centre-of-the-world! Thish club, shtandard bearer Anglo-German culture, what? Great future. Marvellsh!"

He struggled to his feet, and, glass in hand, approached the huge portrait of Hitler that dominated the room.

"Marvellsh man, Hitler," he said. "Great frien' of mine. Makesh us all sit up. Conquer the world. Captain New Zealand to-morrow. Poor ol'Nzealand." He hurled his glass at the portrait. "Heil, ol' boy!" he shouted.

Then the double doors were flung open, to disclose one of the club's most distinguished honorary members, Karl Adolf, Graf von und zu Kissingen-Schwalbach, now a high officer in the S.S. A moment's uneasy silence followed, as he stood in his uniform, motionless, unpleasantly sober. Then Medlincote turned round.

"Schwalbach, my dear fellow," he cried, staggering towards him. "Jusht talking about Adolf. Great frien' of mine. Great fellow. Come in. Tell us more about him. Tell us how he treats the bloody Jews."

He put his two hands on the Count's shoulders. But the Count shook him off, and looked round at the odd assembly, which had begun to laugh rather nervously.

"What is the meaning of this?" he thundered.

Lord John came up, tall, wavy-haired, fatuous.

"Celebration," he said. "Hitler's birthday, or somethin'."

Kissingen-Schwalbach turned on his heel. He shouted an order over the balustrade. Up the wide curved staircase marched fifty Black Guards, armed with revolvers, rubber truncheons, and axes.

Some of the women screamed. The men looked about them in blank amazement. But Medlincote, now lolling on a sofa, had a brainwave of interpretation. "Thash ri', Schwalbach," he shrieked; "give ush demonstration. Show ush how to treat the bloody Jews."

He was silenced with a blow from a truncheon. Ten guards had detached themselves from the ranks with the prearranged purpose, apparently, of apprehending Mr. Medlincote, along with Lord John, Mr. de Courcy, and two other prominent members of the club.

Lord John screamed as his arms were pinioned behind him: "You can't do this to me. You're mad. I'm Lord John St. Neots, and my father is the Duke of Hereford." But all the same he was frogmarched down the stairs.

While the rest of us stood trembling round the walls the remaining Black Guards began systematically to smash up the premises of the club. They broke the chairs, ripped open the sofas, shattered the statues, overturned the vases, flung the wireless set out of the window, shivered the glasses into the fireplace, and occasionally aimed a truncheon blow at one of the cowering male members of the club, while Kissingen-Schwalbach looked satanically on. At length a word of command was given; they re-formed and marched out down the stairs again. Kissingen-Schwalbach remained to give one last contemptuous look at his clubmates, white and staring amid the ruins of their synthetic Valhalla. Then he raised his arm, cried "Heil Hitler!" and left also.

I turned to "Odin". "Several good paragraphs for you here," I remarked. But he clutched my arm, and made a request that came strangely from the mouth of a gossip-writer. "Look, Fenton," he said, "I don't believe they really noticed who I was. Please, please don't tell anyone I was here." Then he rushed out as fast as his legs would carry him.

The wretched mob followed, and some of them were sick on the stairs. I thought I would let them get away first, and lingered for a minute or so in the wrecked lounge. The Germans had done their work thoroughly. Nothing remained unbroken, nothing in place. Only the painting of Adolf Hitler, who gazed steadfastly down upon the broken torso of the Apollo Belvedere.

Now, I reflected, the Terror had reached its consummation. The tide which had risen to engulf all that was worthy in English life was now sucking in the scum. Only Hitler remained, and he made no distinctions.

Chapter Eight

UNDER THE YOKE

IN three weeks it was all over. Not a vestige of liberty survived; not a man remained in office, be he university don or inspector of gas meters, who had not manifested complete submission to the conquerors. The whole machinery of administration, from top to bottom, was seized and made to serve the ends of tyranny; every free association of Britons collapsed or was dissolved. It was a nation of slaves that ate its breakfast in the morning and trudged off to what work there was for it to do.

One fine morning we of the foreign Press (and I was accounted "foreign" now) donned our glossy tall hats and morning coats and went along to what O'Flynn described as the funeral. The Führer, his arm still resting in its sling, had gone back to receive the daemonic acclamations of his own people; but the Reich Commissioner had arrived, in pomp and circumstance, and was about to state his will and pleasure concerning the disposal of the body.

It was the last humiliation to learn that Herr Joachim von Ribbentrop was that Commissioner. One had expected him, that incredibly successful amateur, to remain at his Führer's side, brilliantly directing the next move in the game of world conquest. He should have given England one contemptuous glance, and moved on.

But Joachim von Ribbentrop is a single-minded man. He has a strong and narrow will. He knows how to define his ambitions. To be Foreign Minister of so great an empire that there are no foreign countries left to send ambassadors to would be a huge but Alexandrine triumph; frustration would come with the very completeness of it. There are more solid satisfactions to those wise enough to limit and intensify their desires. And to Joachim von Ribbentrop there could be no sweeter reward than to sit and gloat over the sufferings of the great country that had once stood for everything that he could never understand.

Ribbentrop made a formal entry into London by driving in state, in a carriage with outriders, from Victoria Station, and his vulgar preference for the obvious caused him to choose Buckingham Palace as his official residence. He meant to be a very active Commissioner, and for this purpose must be in the heart of the capital, where all could see and fear him. Pompously he took his seat on the throne before which, not many years ago, he had presented his letters of credence, a *parvenu* among ambassadors.

We attended, then, in morning dress, in a room into which white débutantes had once swept, in another world than this. We sat on rococo chairs, uncomfortably. He kept us waiting, but Dr. Schultz was there, smiling, and obviously trying to make us feel at home. "His Excellency is very busy, but that is understood, yes? Please not to accept discourtesy."

At last there was a stir, and the guards stiffened. "His Excellency the Reich Commissioner!" We struggled to our feet—and the usurper entered, in black uniform, the centre of a group of about half a dozen. He glanced at us, under drooping eyelids, but not as a man to his fellows. He might have been judging cattle.

There was nothing ingratiating in his manner. Schultz and his kind might still be using the old blandishments in their dealings with the foreign Press; it was the tradition of their trade. But Ribbentrop had arrived. He was no longer interested in ladders.

With him were some uniformed German secretaries, alert and cheerful, and three rather strange-looking men in mufti, with walrus moustaches, who did not look German and who hung awkwardly in the background. I had never seen them before.

Schultz presented us individually to the new Lord Protector. He greeted us like a king of the days before kings were expected to smile. He was the same to all of us, even to those whom, when he was Hitler's unofficial agent and still half a champagne peddler, he was pleased enough to meet in London clubs.

Then, when we had all sat down again, he started to explain, in a businesslike way, what he wanted us to know about his régime, and how he expected us to accommodate ourselves to it.

"Under German protection," he said, "Great Britain becomes a totalitarian State, governed by decrees issued in the name of the Reich Commissioner. It is necessary that the foreign Press should appreciate this. The future development of this country will not depend upon political discussions; it will be an expression of the will of the Führer. Consequently, speculation of any kind will no longer form part of visiting Press correspondents' duties. They will learn to beware of any but authorized sources of information.

"As from July the nineteenth, the day on which a vile attempt was made on the life of the Führer, the authority of all magistrates and official bodies in this country and its possessions overseas has been automatically abrogated. It is henceforth an act of subversion, attended by heavy penalties, to communicate with any persons who were members of these bodies for any purpose not strictly personal and private. Certain magistrates and official bodies have, however, by special decree, been restored to their functions during the Führer's pleasure, on taking the oath of loyalty to the Führer. Details of these acts of grace are to be published from time to time in the *London Gazette*."

Some flunkeys rushed in with a map of Great Britain, such as in other circumstances might have inspired youthful patriotism on a schoolroom wall. With relentless pointer the Commissioner divided the proud island into six *Gaue*—North, Midlands, South, London, Scotland, Wales—in each of which, he said, a *Gauleiter*, responsible to him alone, would exercise all administrative authority. Representatives of the *Gauleiter* would be installed in every town and village, where they might be assisted by advisory committees of the local inhabitants. Ireland was to be governed separately by a German "Protector."

The British armed forces had been disarmed and demobilized, but the personnel were "rapidly being recruited into the armed forces of the Reich". All schools, railways, public utility undertakings and banks had become State property, even if privately or municipally owned before; but those persons who had directed them might in some cases be required to continue to do so, subject to control. The old currency would for the time being remain legal tender.

Civil disputes between natives remained subject to the old courts, in so far as these had been confirmed in their functions. All criminal jurisdiction, however, and the settlement of disputes between Reich Germans and natives, had been transferred to the Special Courts set up under the military law. The Special Police had powers to search domiciles, at any hour of day or night, and to take individuals under protective custody. The former Metropolitan police, borough police, and constabulary were at the service of the *Gauleiter* for ordinary police duties.

The State had full powers of expropriation for the common good. An announcement would be made later about the extent to which these powers would be used. It had, however, already been established that the property of all members of the late Warmonger Government was to be confiscated. . . .

The Commissioner had been reading all this from a paper in level, yet monitory, tones. He had said no single word of hope or promise for the future. He had offered nothing, demanded all. His hearers visibly shuddered as he put the paper away.

The Commissioner moved to go. Then his eye fell upon the three queer fellows who had entered so humbly behind him. He turned back and said: "I should have announced that, in accordance with the Führer's express wish, my Advisory Council will be composed entirely of representatives of the British people themselves. Its members are Mr. Smith, representing the employers, Mr. Turner, representing the workers, and Mr. Newton, representing the professions."

He strode out, followed by his suite, leaving the dazed and hangdog Mr. Smith, Mr. Turner, and Mr. Newton at a loss to know whether to go after him. Who were those poor devils? Surely they were our ultimate Quislings, the last feeble representatives of that doomed race of compounders and compromisers who had been our downfall. It was strange to trace them back. There had been Sir John Naker and Professor Evans, so comfortably off, the one in a worldly, the other in an unworldly sense. With them were all Dorman's Unholy Optimists, a varied but such a reassuring tribe. Then, for a brief period, there had been Patrick Rosse, a not ignoble genius, whose appearance and disappearance were equally abrupt. And now there were just Mr. Smith, Mr. Turner, and Mr. Newton, hoping that they could get out of the room before anyone asked them any questions.

Dr. Schultz came into his own again. He tried to reflect

some of the sternness of the Commissioner, but he could not bring himself to abandon altogether his professional geniality. "Well, gentlemen, thank you for your arrival. We understand the other much better now, I suppose?" He bowed us out.

We had come in taxis, which in our station of life is a ceremonial mode of conveyance, but most of us walked back. Imagine our little heterogeneous group, top-hatted, walking along the Mall, attracting mild remark among the listless passers-by, and feeling like tourists in some great dead city. Behind us the white palace, with the Commissioner's Swastika flag flying where the Royal Standard ought to be; on the left, St. James's, where (a long time ago, it seemed now) the pit had suddenly opened before the craven rulers of the nation; and, all among the trees, those imperial towers which still stood up so boldly and yet now were a hollow shell.

We discussed the prospects of our work in London under the new régime. Was it worth while to stay? Did Ribbentrop mean that we were expected to become mere agents for transmitting German communiqués?

It was a Brazilian journalist who persuaded most of us to hang on while we could. We had crowded, almost without knowing it, into a little public house in the Strand, where the astonished landlord, noticing our unaccustomed appearance, feared that we were some new infliction from Germany, and was pathetically anxious to please. All the other customers drank up and respectfully left.

"After all," said Senhor Diaz, "we may possibly be allowed to describe, if not to interpret. In our descriptions we can be a little—subtle. If Ribbentrop is going to incorporate the British economic system into that of the Reich it will be a great newspaper story. And if we can't send it, we can save it up and write it when we get home."

There was sense in this, and then someone remarked quietly that while we remained the Germans might make some show of moderating the cruelties of the régime. That alone made it our duty to stay.

So, as the landlord rushed up anxiously with another round of drinks, we made a kind of pact—to stay as long as it was reasonably safe to stay, to get all the truth we could past the censorship, and, if we reached home, to set down on paper everything we had been able to observe. I have not yet kept the last part of the bargain, and this book is no serious attempt to do so; but one day I hope to be able to place at the disposal of historians and economists a mass of strange facts, which, bewildering as they are to me, may be justly interpreted by them.

It is, however, easy to distinguish two aspects of Herr von Ribbentrop's régime. It ministers to a sadistic desire for revenge and moral vandalism, a brutish urge to destroy what is not understood; but at the same time it has achieved a miracle of political organization—the merging of the whole mercantile economy of Britain into the self-sufficient economy of the Reich.

The first aspect is not one to dwell upon, unless by pathologists. To the ordinary mind it would not be instructive, and it would be exceedingly unpleasant, to follow Ribbentrop on those morbid excursions on which he tried to pull to pieces, with his own fingers, the inmost souls of the men he hated. His notorious visits to Mr. Churchill and Mr. Eden at Godalming concentration camp; his attendance *incognito* at East End pogroms; his cat and mouse game with the panting, perspiring Sir John Naker—these are best forgotten, if they can be. So, too, are his deliberate affronts to the feelings of the vanquished, as when Hitler superseded Nelson in Trafalgar Square and the German Eagle swung like a blasphemous rood beneath the dome of St. Paul's. But there is just this to be said. Ribbentrop's evil propensities never achieved complete satisfaction. He might rant and bully and mock, but still in the sorrowful glances that were raised to him, by the once great as well as by the obscure, there was always the sign of that inmost citadel of the spirit that no human savagery can destroy. The consciousness of this must have followed Ribbentrop down his dark career, and driven him to even worse, but ever vain, excesses.

But there remains the other aspect of his régime, the exploitation of all the resources of Britain—a policy brilliantly, almost incredibly, successful. In the slough of his moral degradation the Reich Commissioner never lost the mastery of those ruthlessly efficient methods by which the Nazis, from being a little conspiratorial group in Munich, have by relentless stages come to dominate the world. He had clever lieutenants, no doubt, men like Himmler (for a time), Schacht, the inevitable Seyss-Inquart, and a new star, Fritz Ostenhammer, the Commissioner for Industry. But the Reich Commissioner himself can fairly claim the major share of the credit for a very remarkable achievement.

The devilishly complete subjugation of the whole machine of national life—the preliminary programme so frigidly announced to us in Buckingham Palace—happened exactly as planned. One must imagine that, months before, a minor but fanatical Nazi in Darmstadt was told to brush up his English and his knowledge of Fen drainage because he would one day be entrusted with the administrative oversight of the Isle of Ely; well, sure enough, the day arrived when this gentleman, properly escorted, presented himself at Wisbech, showed his authority to the clerk to the county council and the mayor, and got to work simultaneously on the necessary purges and on a pet plan for deepening the outfall of the Nene. It happened just like that. One day you might be in exasperating correspondence with Mr. Jones, of the local electrical undertaking, about additional power for your factory; by the next, you had received a businesslike letter stating that an engineer would be calling on you on Wednesday, and signed by the Herr Oberelektrizitätstundige Schmidt.

"There is one thing about these Germans," nervously remarked the heads of big business, trying to whistle up each other's courage; "they do get things done." They do indeed. Once they had gained control of the Board of Admiralty, as of Snoring Parva Parish Council, they passed rapidly on to the next phase. They made it clear that they had not come to England merely to teach the art of efficient administration. They showed us how simple it was to turn us into slaves.

We were to be a German colony—and a colony in the old, bad sense. All our resources, of men and material, were to be at the service of the German State, without regard to human rights or dignity. Our very lives were to depend on their usefulness to Hitler.

Overnight we were swallowed by the Nazi autarky. Lenin had not led a greater revolution than that. Masters and men, borrowers and lenders, buyers and sellers—in a moment these various relationships which had so completely governed our lives were dissolved and rebuilt into a State socialism designed to serve the needs of another empire.

The City's collapse was complete. Its leading strings of world finance suddenly went slack; an invisible wall arose to isolate it from the non-German world; and the pound sterling became a meaningless cipher. Fortunes vanished, shares ceased to be quoted. That vast system of credit on which had floated the trade of more than half the world burst like a toy balloon. Henceforth, the Square Mile was to be but a minor Nazi counting-house.

Thus England became a poor country, without those great financial resources which had enabled her to live like a lord among the nations. It was no longer a question of juggling with stocks and shares and sitting back and receiving dividends from foreign parts; all that now could be done was to dig the coal from the bowels of the earth, smelt the ore, forge the weapons, faster and ever faster; and then to barter them for the bare necessities of life. A large part of the great middle-class, who had been working all this while in the artificial world of credit, found themselves with nothing to do but work miserably with their hands.

The cosmopolitan financiers had miscalculated. They thought that Germany would take over British capital resources, and make use of them in an orthodox way. They thought that they themselves could batten on the new world as on the old. They forgot that international confidence depended on international security, and that paper relationships and paper wealth mean nothing to Nazis on the march.

Finance capital, in fact, was doomed. The world's new masters were to grow rich, not by lending money and keeping the peace, but by making war and seizing the booty. The bomber and the police machine gun had confounded the economists.

As far as Great Britain was concerned the Nazi aim was simple. Here was a highly industrialized country, organized for foreign trade, and having certain mineral resources that Germany lacked. Let her continue to produce, let the products be bartered abroad for whatever Germany might want, and let all the surplus raw materials be sent to Germany. The whole of British industry was to be reorganized to further these ends. Dr. Schacht instituted his Three Years' Plan, and effectively abolished the old commercial criterion of whether an enterprise was likely to pay. The notion of profit, like that of taxation, soon became obsolete in England; all that happened was that England produced the goods, and Germany either used or bartered them.

The industrialists, like the financiers, were bitterly disappointed. "The Germans can't do without us," they had said. "We must strike a bargain." But the Germans could very well do without them, or, at least, compel the more intelligent of them to accept subordinate executive positions in their own businesses. One does not spend ten years building a self-sufficient war economy without learning some of the arts of socialist organization.

The final blow to the possessing classes came when sterling was declared no longer legal tender. Thus at one blow all monetary savings disappeared; even the well-to-do were then utterly dependent on the Nazis for the means of subsistence. They must perform the tasks allotted to them, or starve.

And what of the workers? Slowly their standard of living was forced down to the lowest tolerable level. The real value of wages decreased, and hours grew longer. The quality of food deteriorated. Butter and even margarine became scarce, bananas and other tropical fruit were unobtainable, and for a time at least (most cruel blow of all) tobacco and tea were off the market.

The trade unions, of course, disappeared, and whether Mallory's young friend at Transport House appreciated the new labour régime when it was actually imposed under the kindly eye of Dr. Ley I cannot tell. The British Labour Front produced neither bread nor circuses. Its officials, as far as I could gather, merely advised the Government on what was the least food on which the British workman could subsist, and it never troubled about May Day parades. Every now and again, however, it sent to Berlin mock resolutions of gratitude and loyalty to the Führer.

But poverty and long hours are no absolute bar to happiness. Those who were in love, or happily married, or fortunate in their children, might still have made a corner of their lives worth living, without the cakes and ale. But Fate seemed to know no mercy. Britain, according to the Three Years' Plan, was overpopulated, while Germany was still mobilized. What was there easier, then, than to take the surplus British workmen and drive them, like the helots they were, into German factories, leaving, for economy's sake, their wives and children behind? The Polish harvest, too, was more important than the British, and Poland was depopulated: once again, the wonders of modern transport organization could be invoked, and a slave ship from Hull reach Danzig with a thousand British farm labourers battened below hatches.

Here is a mighty supple instrument of tyranny. If a workman shows signs of political activity, or if the Nazi overseer for any reason does not like him, it is the simplest thing in the world to have him conscripted for service oversea. If a whole workshop is suspected of sabotage, or falls in any way below the standard of production demanded, a little bookkeeping at the Central Employment Exchange will suffice for one man in every ten to be sent to Galicia. In that case the hold tightens, for there is no-one but regards the ten in Galicia as anything but hostages for the hundred who remain behind.

It does not take many secret police to hold down England. One in every factory, helped by a few spies; one in every group of villages; one for every block of streets. Each is protected by an invisible human screen—by the score or so of men, women, and children who would pay with their lives were any desperate attempt to be made on his. Each knows how to corrupt still further the frightened little group he dominates. Each serves at once his own greedy ends and his Führer's.

The revolution is complete. The purpose of the humblest life has been changed. One day an historian, in possession of all the facts, will draw a complete picture of the monstrous efficiency with which the Ribbentrop régime has established itself in every strategic position in the course of its subjugation of a people. I confess it has bewildered me; the impact was so tremendous that I never got any real bird's-eye view of what was happening. Power and authority changed hands; old principles of economics were shown to be irrelevant; a regime that everyone hated had everything its own way. What I chiefly remember is such a case as that of Mrs. Jenkins, our charwoman. She was an excellent soul, who had brought up a large family in thrift and cleanliness, and launched them all in good jobs. One son had been killed at Dunkirk, but at the time she had felt proud of the sacrifice. Now she had reached the age at which she might have hoped to take things more easily and enjoy her port and lemon in peace. But the currency laws deprived her of her few savings, two of her four remaining sons were transported to Germany, and her husband was rapidly succumbing to diabetes because the supply of insulin had been stopped. Life had become hard and even tragic for her, yet she dared not discuss her troubles with her friends; and when she got home she could not even make herself a cup of tea.

Chapter Nine

VALHALLA IN SYDENHAM

IT sounds incredible, but von Holtz's forecast came true; in September, one year after the peace of Nuremberg, Hitler duly appointed London to be "the Vienna of the West". It all happened at a Cultural Congress in a bigger and uglier post-war Albert Hall, which was one of the saddest and dullest congresses I have ever attended. I remember when I came away from it walking most disconsolately through the lifeless streets, and thinking what a strange thing it must be to be a dictator, and yet not to be able to touch anything good and true without making it stop or go wrong.

The London I had come to six short years before had been a *Weltstadt*, a mainspring of world civilization. It had been an imperial capital, the source and inspiration of good government in a thousand corners of the globe. Its financial organization had governed that immense system which allowed railways to be built in Argentina and power-houses in Turkey. It had been the place where conflicting interests met and found their levels. Above all it had been teeming with ideas, societies, and causes which, working themselves out through the whole body of human endeavour, had leavened the mass and given zest and purpose to life.

To-day, in this "Vienna of the West", there were no spontaneous movements, no grand personal ambitions, no fads and fancies, no enthusiasms; there was only a desire to stand well with the authorities. There were no people struggling ahead with their life's work in founding hospitals or advocating dress reform; there were only government officials. Instead of the Band of Hope there was the Greater Reich Anti-Alcoholism Bureau; instead of the Sawyer's Arms Sick and Dividing Club there was the Hampstead Centre for Compulsory Winter Help. No meeting, however small, could be held without a police licence; and it would have taken a brave and importunate man to organize a pigeon-fanciers' society or a chess club. But the sad thing was that, even had the right of free association been granted, there would have been few who had the heart to take advantage of it.

A great city lives through its sectional interests. Kindred spirits seek each other out and form groups, wise or foolish. The little wheels revolve, movements grow, the enormous human mass becomes spiritually as well as economically mobilized. In such conditions town life is tolerable; there is more in society than buying and selling and the deadening limits of family or boarding-house life. But when this natural diversification of interests is prevented, as under the Nazis, the sparkling crystals break down, the mass coagulates, and can be stirred only by crude and violent means. In Berlin there were marches and parades, and all the horrible stimulants of mass hysteria. London was now denied even this substitute for life; it could be moved only by fear.

The spectacle of eight million people together living lives mainly actuated by fear is no pleasant one. Nor, fortunately, is it common, for the circumstances which produce fear usually also give ground for such compensating emotions as the joy of struggle, a sense of comradeship, the excitement caused by external change, or the self-expressive satisfaction of martyrdom. But these sensations were all strange to the dull London crowds of that autumn. As for the struggle, it had been abandoned; and, far from there being a new sense of comradeship in adversity, the hateful tendency to curry favour by informing against one's neighbours was beginning to rear its head. Since there was no resistance, there was no romance, no material for boyish literature; life in the concentration camps was dull as well as painful. There were many martyrs, but they moved forward not as a glorious army.

The Berlin correspondent of the *Wellington Courier*, A. P. Hodges, passed through London on his way home on leave. He had just paid a visit to Prague, and he noted the apparent absence in England of that fierce inward flame of patriotism that still burned among the Czechs. "Heaven knows why they still hope," he said, "but they do, whereas you here seem to have thrown in even your moral hand straight away." One explanation we thought of was that the Czechs had little to reproach themselves with, while the British had everything; and we agreed that the British had surrendered much more in the way of hopes, ambitions, and ideals.

Except for the fear of mean but crippling personal disasters (such as losing one's job or money or being beaten by the Brownshirts), what was there to think about? There was no longer any honourable career for oneself or one's sons—nothing to do but accept a subordinate position in a Prussian administration or attempt to make money out of the situation (and then not to be allowed to spend it as one wished). Politics no longer existed, either to be engaged in or discussed; the law had become yet another instrument of tyranny; science and learning also were prostituted; and even the consecrated calling of medicine was beginning to be misused in the horrible interests of National Socialist "eugenics". It was virtually impossible for an Englishman to render any but menial service to his fellow men.

This was sufficiently demoralizing, but added to it there was that complete devastation of intellectual life which deprived people of all but dangerous forms of escapism. The Vienna of the West was singularly devoid of mental stimulus; the German and English "cultures", so rudely united, proved a barren pair.

Everyone, of course, was busy learning German, and to unwilling pupils this was a severe enough task. "We have the greatest respect for the language of Shakespeare," shrieked Dr. Goebbels at the Cultural Congress, using an unpleasant guttural form of it, "but its rôle as a universal tongue has passed by. In course of time it will become a dead language

—a fruitful field of research, perhaps, for our great German scholars, and a medium in which certain poetry may continue to be written, but no language of practical affairs. A generation of Anglo-Germans will arise who will know it not, except as a means of recapturing, as a mental discipline, the spirit of that distracted world which waited it knew not for what—which waited, as we now know, for Adolf Hitler." (Regulation cheers.) "The English tongue will become sacred in the lecture-room, but it will be forgotten in the market and the street. It will certainly"—and here Dr. Goebbels raised an admonitory finger and was greeted by the most frantic cheering from the Brownshirts—"it will certainly be no language for political discussion."

It was announced that official German translations would be approved of all the great English classics, like Shakespeare, Byron, and Wilde, and that in course of time the original versions would be confined to the learned libraries. No English would be taught to children now entering school for the first time, and in another five years all public examinations would be conducted in German. The *People's Observer*, now the only remaining daily newspaper, would in a year or so become the *Völkischer Beobachter* again, with only a small English supplement for the "illiterate". Hitler himself, though lapped in the Tudor traditions of Hampton Court, proposed not to burden his great mind with one word of the captive tongue, except the three with which, of a hideous incongruity, he sometimes concluded his venomous speeches—"God bless you".

Such was the conquerors' linguistic programme, one of the most savage known to history. It will defeat itself, for to proscribe a great and noble tongue which still flourishes in other parts of the world is to invest it with enormous revolutionary power. In London soon one will have only to whisper, in English, "Pass the salt", to utter a challenge; "I beg your pardon" will be a defiance; and "Thanks, chum" will stand for Harry, England, and St. George.

Still, there we were, then, learning the Common Terminations and the Declension of Adjectives, and feeling all the time as though we had been kept in. What was there to distract us? The theatre was dead; apart from certain propagandist plays, which those who had accepted official employment felt bound to see, every theatre left open was running a revival of some sort, usually Shakespeare or an Edwardian musical comedy. The cinemas were used only for holding hands in the dark; no-one looked at the screen. Artists hesitated to paint; they waited to be quite sure what was decadent and what was not. There was nothing to talk about, nothing to look forward to, nothing to read.

So the one common resource, naturally, was gossip, often the kind of gossip that was capable of taking a very sinister turn indeed. One would not have thought that the sneak, the denouncer, would ever play an important part in English life; but there it is, it has happened, and we in New Zealand must try to understand rather than condemn.

Imagine forty million people, the greater part of them acknowledging in their hearts little more than the pagan virtues and sentimentalities, suddenly bereft of the symbols and fetishes which had held together their common life and governed their social behaviour. They are faced, almost to a man, with unbelievable adversity. Their standard of living is forced down, but that is the least of their troubles. They are entirely without security; on any day major disaster may overtake them, in the form of unemployment, imprisonment and torture, loss of house and home, separation from their families, transportation, and even death from lack of food. Every horror which has in the centuries swept over the patient masses of China is in a month or two confronting a people among whom respect for private rights, as well as pride of race, has been developed to the highest degree. Each man is left to face his particular misery alone; he is denied the right of consulting with his fellows, and there is none to speak for him in high places. All human standards are cast down; a man's individual conscience alone can be heard above the confusion.

How many of us can swear that, deprived of our accustomed moral support, we would consistently obey that voice? The ship sinks, the boat drill is pronounced useless by those who should have led it. Is it not then every man for himself, or at least for his loved ones?

Left alone in cottage parlours, suburban sitting-rooms, or the faded drawing-rooms of country houses, fathers and mothers wonder about the future of their children. They may forget about their country, for it belongs to the past, and there is no means left to express their loyalty to it. But John and Joan and Robert belong to the future, if the Germans will only let them survive. Maybe, when they are grown, they will win their country back again. But if they can't get enough food, or if they are transported to Poland, or if the hospital refuses their admission for the operation for appendicitis, all patriotic dreams will be in vain. So it is as well to co-operate, for the time being; and if one's old friend next door seems to be a little obstinate, and behaves in a way which may bring down the Nazi wrath on the whole street or village, he is really not doing much good, either to himself or to others. Perhaps the Gestapo agent will be asking questions about it. Well, we can at least make it clear to him that we have nothing to do with subversive activities next door. And suppose he drops a hint about "protection" for us and the children, might we not tell him the little we know? After all, it is not sufficient to condemn the man. . . .

This, dear civilized readers, is temptation indeed, and the armoury against it is often pathetically inadequate. Think of those obsolete weapons, which no ammunition will now fit—the public school spirit, trade union solidarity, intellectual integrity, respectability, family pride. Not one of them now functions. It remains to be shown what deeper resources there are in a once Christian England. Who now carries the shield of faith and the sword of the Spirit? Who has put on, in the evil day, the panoply of God?

The external practice of religion survives. At first sight, perhaps, it bears the repellent aspect of a corpse, like a number of other institutions that have incongruously lingered on in Nazi England. Just as Hitler's "law" is still largely administered under ancient forms, by new judges in old wigs; just as the universities, though mere institutes of prostituted and *vergoebbelt* learning, largely retain their inherited organization of colleges and terms: so the Anglican Church remains, still drawing its tithes and husbanding its endowments. The Nazis evidently regard it as a stabilizing influence, in the new as in the old State; and they only ask that preachers who allude too pointedly to the rulers of the darkness of this world should be taken for a time under "protective custody". The Nonconformist churches they are less sure about; so much might be going on behind the multifarious façades of Dissent. A system of registration has accordingly been established. Services may be held only in the larger churches and at appointed times, in the presence of a Nazi inspector—and woe betide the local preacher who introduces the slightest reference to current politics into what is licensed as an orthodox exposition of Lutheran or Calvinist theology, as the case may be. The smaller and less explicable denominations have impatiently been told that they must merge into one or other of the larger. It is hard if you think that you and your few friends alone compose the Elect to be told by a policeman to join the lost congregation in the next street, but Hitlerism and sectarianism are clearly at opposite poles. The Salvation Army has been demobilized, or at any rate has lost its uniforms and its right to march; Christian Science is considered "politically unreliable". But the only groups that are actively persecuted and expropriated are the Quakers and the Papists; both are uncomfortable people for Nazis to melt outside a concentration camp.

But church services under the British captivity have, as I have admitted, a first appearance of insincerity. The formal readings in the parish churches, the stiff, united worship in the chapels under the eye of a Nazi spy, the mumbling of masses in barns and warehouses are, on the surface, unconnected with any protest against the tyranny to which Englishmen not only submit but in which they to some extent take part. They are certainly no revolutionary assemblages, and the tocsin will never be rung by the curate of St. Simon's and St. Jude's up the street. But remember this. They provide the only pretext, not imposed by the Nazis, upon which Englishmen can with relative impunity meet together. It would be possible to argue that, if the country has been saved from complete degradation, if there are still remnants of honour and restraint and some gleams of charity among a people more cruelly and hopelessly persecuted than any in history, this is because when they meet it is in God's name.

I returned once or twice to Smithers's church, the Congregational one at Tanner's End. There was my old friend, the Rev. Mr. Brownlow, whose flock, apart from being swollen, binder the "rationalization scheme", by a few Peculiar Baptists of the neighbourhood, was nearly twice as big as it was before. There, too, was the Nazi spy, in his special pew; people were quite kind to him, and often asked him home to Sunday dinner. The service was purely devotional, with not the obliquest reference to politics that I could detect, except the general implication of Christian teaching that the State is not exempt from the laws and punishments of God. Though an outsider, and uninitiate, I soon became conscious of the impelling attraction of that simple, unwontedly formal, service. The people there, so tragic in their worldly circumstances, seemed to come to stand silently round a deep and healing well. In the old days, when they could debate their pacifism freely and quote the Bible in support of political shibboleths, such a simile would never have occurred to me.

After the service was over, and one had shaken hands with the parson at the door, one walked out again into the desert. And what a desert it was! The congregation broke up rapidly —not to have done so might have provoked a truncheon charge by the police—and each little family group hurried back to its shabby home, an Englishman's castle no longer. The shuttered streets were soon deserted, and to me they presented the most dismal and hopeless prospect that I have ever been able to conceive. It was a London suburb and it was Sunday, but, beyond all the suspension of healthy human activity which that statement implies, there was a deeper and more terrible stillness. It was not sleep but death.

And yet the Germans went on with that Cultural Congress at which London was solemnly named "Vienna of the West". Vienna, we knew, was the "cultural capital of the Reich", but not, so far as we had heard, a particularly effective one. Hodges told me that it had never been duller since the period of hunger which followed the Four Years' War, and that all that was happening was that a group of Nazi scholars imported from North Germany were editing a great *Encyclopaedia Germanica* there. However, dictators can't do without culture, so we resigned ourselves to becoming a second Vienna, and were not surprised to learn that the central manifestation was to be a concrete building called the Valhalla of Nordic Virtues, which was to be set up where the Crystal Palace used to be. Hitler himself was said to have designed it, and this may have been so, for, from the drawings, it was to be an immense structure, domed and pyramided, ten times uglier than the Crystal Palace. As to what was to go on there, arrangements were still somewhat vague, but as time went on an odd assortment of intellectuals emerged who were willing, it seemed, for security and a competence, to carve the right statues, paint the right "murals", and compose the right odes for forging the new culture of Germany's western fringe. Their only problem was to know in what proportions they should mix Anglo-Saxon motives, the baroque picturesqueness of southern Germany, and the vulgar grandiosity associated with all modern dictatorships. Otherwise they went their silly way in peace, ministering duly to the Führer's megalomania. They were our intellectual Quislings, and it would have been easy to be satirical at their expense. But it would not have been amusing, because no-one took them seriously, and most of the German high officials forgot all about them. After conquest, cultural propaganda takes a back place, with practical people.

One day a party of the foreign Press were taken to see the site being prepared on Sydenham Hill. The man who showed us round turned out to be von Holtz himself. I had met him several times since 19th July, and, as was everyone's way in a time when principles were being shed one by one, I had allowed the general treachery of his countrymen towards my Motherland to remain unremarked. Tacitly excluding this subject from conversation, I found I could talk to him without embarrassment; he, on his part, affected at first a somewhat deprecatory tone, as though to suggest that his Führer and he regretted that the character of the vanquished had proved such that the victors were compelled to proceed to rather extreme measures. But as time went on I thought I detected, on his not unfrank countenance, a growing trace of disillusion, perhaps even of frustration. Certainly, I recalled, the picture he had drawn as we talked together on the roof of Bush House in May had not come to life. On a soil so heavily trampled, so stained with blood, it never could; the fine flower of Anglo-German culture, that von Holtz had thought to stick proudly in his buttonhole, would never bloom at all.

I kept pondering about this man as he led us somewhat despondently over the squelchy ground, pointing out where the giant statue of Odin was to rise, and where that of Adolf. I wondered if he had been really sincere last May, and had indeed expected a golden millennium, Teutonic maybe, but none the less idealistic and principled, pseudo-Kiplingesque. If so, he might be representative of a growing conservative influence in Germany that was reacting against the diseased inhumanity of the gang now in control. I fancied I had met other highly placed Nazis to whom similar views might, by the observant, be ascribed. Was it possible that decency and restraint would one day emerge again among the Germans, that horror and disgust would grow at what had been committed, and that some clumsy, materialistic, but yet tolerable mode of civilization would return?

I sounded von Holtz discreetly, looking anxiously for any signs of a conflict within him. I thought I descried them, and rejoiced.

We had reached the site of the Triumphal Way, a great vista to be closed with a group of statuary showing "Britannia being Received into the Nordic Family of Nations". A plaster model of the group was already in position, and from the bottom of the avenue it looked extraordinarily like the Laocoön.

"You'll feel quite at home, von Holtz," I said, "when all this is finished. Isn't it modelled on the Führer's new layout of the Tiergarten?" He agreed that there would be a resemblance. "In fact," I went on, "London ought soon to be indistinguishable from Berlin, or, at least, from any fairly important German provincial town. It doesn't look as though Britannia is to be allowed to make any very remarkable contribution of her own to the Nordic Family of Nations."

He took me by the arm, apart from the others. For a

moment I thought he was about to make a confession, the kind of confession that one likes to dream of disillusioned Nazis making. He looked stern and anxious. I prepared to assume the part of father confessor, and thought out in advance my little speech of absolution.

"You are thinking of what we said on the roof of the former Embassy," he began, stiffly. "I said then that there was nothing our two nations could not do together. I said they needed each other to face the tasks of the modern world. I believed there would be a great cultural revival in England. I had a great and noble vision, and I thought the Führer shared it too. But now I see I was wrong."

He paused. "Splendid, foolish, misguided man!" I thought. "If there are enough like you in Germany there is still hope for the future happiness of the world."

"Yes," he went on, "I was wrong. As you see, I was wrong. Britannia contributes nothing to the common stock. And why? Because she is undisciplined, irresolute, unprepared for the blessings the Führer is ready to shower upon her. Dazzling opportunities are presented to her, and she turns the other way. Instead of being quickened into life, she swoons and faints. Germany has allied herself to a corpse."

So much for my own daydream. I swallowed hard.

"Forgive me," he continued, as fiercely as ever, "forgive me for talking to you like this. But you are a New Zealander, and I think you cannot appreciate how tragic all this seems to a European. I tell you the Führer is going ahead with this project with a sob in his heart. He knew from the very beginning what some of us did not know—that a disciplined nation cannot effectively co-operate with an undisciplined one. He knew that he would first have to fight over again in England the fight he won in Germany. But he will not fail in his respect for a daughter Nordic nation, however debased. The Valhalla will be inaugurated even in an unregenerate Britain, and then it can stand as an inspiration in the struggle to come."

A little Japanese journalist had approached us, and overheard some of this strange outburst. When I walked away to conceal my mortification, he stepped beside me. "Poor old von Holtz," he said. "He has been getting worse lately. His trouble is that he had hoped to marry an earl's daughter, and finds now that nobody would be the least bit interested if he did."

I had not realized before what a dull place England must seem to its German conquerors, now that it had collapsed.

After this it seemed a relief to get an invitation from the

Warden and Fellows of St. Mary's College to attend that odd form of students' reunion dinner which is known in Oxford as a Gaudy. I had lost touch with St. Mary's when I returned to New Zealand after my Rhodes Scholarship had expired, and I accepted the invitation with some interest. Elizabeth and the child went to stay with friends—a necessary precaution in those days—and, after I had notified the Press Bureau of my temporary absence, I made the familiar journey from Paddington, and entered my old rooms over the archway in good time to dress for dinner. They looked unchanged: the afternoon sunlight fell across the same old cushions in the window-seat; the bulky and battered Victorian furniture abode in its place, and the arm-chair with a loose spring still kept watch beside the fireplace. There were fewer books on the pseudo-Gothic dresser, however, and they had taken on a new and sickly complexion. German primers and elementary textbooks were to be expected, but a frothy and rhetorical work on the *Duties of Nordic Manhood* was new to me, and so was the ponderous and three-volumed *History of the Germanic Family of Nations*, although I had heard of its publication by that repository of crank racial theory, Colonel Gregory-Smith. Books indicating the actual studies of the present occupant of these rooms were remarkably few; as far as I could judge, his main course was some form of civil engineering, an odd line for a St. Mary's man to take.

My explorations were interrupted by the entry of my old scout, Blackett, who, after the manner of his kind, made me respectfully welcome and succeeded in conveying to me not only that he remembered me perfectly but that I belonged to a select and favoured generation of undergraduates. "Well, how's the College these days?" I inquired, fatuously but inevitably. "Very quiet, sir," said Blackett. "There's a lot of German gentlemen here now, sir, and they are a very serious lot, even in their drink. Hard-working too in a way."

"What way is that?" I asked. "Are they all learning English?" "No, sir," said Blackett shortly. "Soldiering is their line of study. Proper drill'all the College is these days." "But this gentleman," I said, pointing to the books. "Ah, he's a real gentleman, he is," said Blackett hastily. "He's learning plumbing. You see he's a . . . well, he's not a German gentleman, if you'll excuse me." He looked at me a little anxiously. I understood and changed the subject. I had thought of calling on my old tutor before dinner, and asked if he was still in his old rooms. A wooden look came over Blackett's face. "No, sir," he said distantly. "Mr. Martens was taken very ill after some German gentleman in uniform had called on him.

Some trouble over a lecture I did hear it was. But he's had what they call a nervous breakdown since then, and they've taken him away." I thought of the austere, almost contemptuous front which Martens had presented to the world, and I felt a little sick at the thought of that nervous breakdown.

Blackett had disappeared into the bedroom and was laying out my clothes. "Well, I hope I see some familiar faces," I said, following him in.

"There's been a lot of changes lately, sir," he muttered. "Mind you, I'm not complaining. Of course with the new Warden it's natural that there should be a lot of German gentlemen in the Senior Common Room." "What's the new Warden's name?" I asked, a little faintly. "Dr. Perchoven, sir," said Blackett, disappearing.

After these preliminaries, I was not surprised by the scene in the hall. At the high table the conversation was in German, and there were two officers present in full uniform. Dr. Perchoven proved to be a square-headed, close-cropped man of middle-age who peered occasionally down the room through thick-lensed steel spectacles. Half of the dons of my time had disappeared, and the remainder, except for a hurried, almost furtive greeting to old students, were remarkably taciturn. They were ignored by their new German colleagues, and seemed thankful for this mercy.

At my table English was spoken, but it was a very silent company. Two places away from me was one of the new German Fellows, an enthusiastic ex-leader of German Youth, who embarked in perfect English on a discourse on the anomalies and futilities of the English system of education before it had been "leavened with our vital German culture". His remarks were ostensibly addressed to his *vis-à-vis*, but since everybody was so silent they took on much of the character of a lecture, and continued, interrupted only by hasty mouthfuls, until the end of dinner. I knew neither of my neighbours, and neither of them appeared at all anxious to talk. It was one of the most uncomfortable meals I have ever eaten, and I could not imagine why the authorities had found it necessary to convene such an assembly. This, however, was explained when the Warden rose to make his speech with the dessert. Whatever may have been his branch of learning, it was certainly not linguistics, and his remarks, although delivered in the "dead language" of English out of courtesy—or pity—for his hearers, were not distinguished for their fluency.

St. Mary's, we understood him to say, had been one of the most richly endowed colleges of the university. But where had this wealth come from? It had been drained ruthlessly from the rich estates which the college owned. What had a place of learning to do with such wealth and such land? he asked, and answered himself firmly: Nothing. "Such gold", he said, "was for no useful purpose. It was as you say the idle talent, and much good was left undone through the avarice of the collegers. This have I changed. This gold, this land has St. Mary to the Führer dedicated, and it shall from now for the good of all, not of a few, be utilized." He paused for the applause which was given with enthusiasm by the German members of his audience and more tepidly by some of the others. "Now", he continued with gusto, "it shall be the duty of the former student his Alma Mater to support. You, gentlemen, vill haf that privilege." His spectacles flashed in the candlelight as he beamed round the hall. In a little while, we were told, the Bursar, Professor Hoffstein, would come round with blank cheque forms. On these we would write what we would gladly give towards the annual support of the foundation. "Nor let the sum be insignificant," the Warden boomed. "Ve Germans haf the quality of free-handed gifting, and the miser is not by us beloved."

There was an uncomfortable stir as he concluded. Everyone was calculating how much and how little he could give to avert the wrath to come. I had decided that, miser or no miser, two hundred marks was my limit. They could not expect much more from a journalist. As I sat waiting for the Bursar to reach me on his round I suddenly caught sight of a familiar and friendly face. What is more, it was smiling at me, and that, on such an evening, was an event in itself. It was the face of David Grant, a red-haired Scot from Aberdeen. I had not seen him since the night when, our finals over and celebrated, he had cornered me after dinner and delivered a lecture on the predestined damnation of all who turned their mother-tongue into a course for study—an offence of which I had been guilty. He had been a scientist, and was going on, I understood, to a specialized course in agriculture, "in order to teach the misguided peasantry of this degenerate land how to make a proper use of the earth they till". I had not seen him from that ribald night to this.

When we were released from our ordeal in the hall he came over to me. "You'll come round to my rooms?" he asked. "I have a modicum of whisky there, and we'll just get the taste of this collation out of our mouths." It was with difficulty that I refrained from looking over my shoulder, and he saw my movement. "Ah well," he said, smiling, "we will rather continue the conviviality which has been so remarkable a feature of the evening so far. Allow me to introduce you to Professor Leitch, now of Edinburgh, and a distinguished member of this college long before you or I set foot in it." I shook hands with a little, lame man whom I had scarcely noticed behind David's burly shoulder. He looked up at me as I was introduced, and with that movement ceased to be insignificant. He had the bluest and most brilliant eyes that I have ever seen in any man, and they held mine in a steady and appraising examination. He said very little, and when we were presently seated round the fire it was David who did the talking. At least I thought it was, but I gradually realized that I was being led on to express my own opinions with more freedom than I had for months. I stopped abruptly, cursing myself for the folly of giving myself away to two strangers. There was a moment's silence, and then the old professor, who had been gazing into the fire, spoke without looking at me. He had a low, clear and rather beautiful voice and its very sound was reassuring.

"You need have no fear, Mr. Fenton," he said. "David here has been cross-examining you a wee bit stringently, but he's no informer. Neither am I. This hip of mine was smashed in Dalkeith camp last July."

I murmured some sort of disclaimer and apology, but he continued:

"You do right to be fearful. There's no security in idle talk these days. But David's talk was not idle. He was as anxious to find how you looked at things, as you were to know his purpose, when you realized which way the talk was leading. But I fancy there's three honest men met together for once." He looked round at me with a warm smile, and the last of my fears vanished.

Then the talk continued in real earnest. They were both, I learnt, agricultural specialists, and as such respected and valued by the German authorities, who saw the importance of making full use of the soil of their new possession. "We've got something they want, do you see?" said David with a grin, "and unfortunately for them it's not confiscatable. They've found no way yet of grafting a good Scots brain into a Prussian headpiece." The professor's sojourn in a concentration camp had been due to false information laid by a German student at their research station, who planned by this means to be given the directorship. He got his wish, but he very soon found that the presence of the professor was indispensable to the work, and had him released to serve in a subordinate capacity. "But the new director's not so comfortable as he thought to be," remarked David. "We don't give him any handle; boys at the station are not demonstrative, but they have a quiet way of making him feel himself superfluous."

That, I learnt, was generally the position of the Germans in Scotland. Except for a few outbursts in the big cities, which were repressed by typical methods during the Terror, Scotland had met the invasion with a dour silence which was by no means acceptance. Brutality had been met with a stubborn power to endure injustice and injury. The fulsome outpourings of the German "cultural front" on the close relationship between the Scottish and the German cultures had been snubbed with a stony glare and a devastating silence. "There was a havering body", commented David, "that told me the Germans had the same word for kirk as we had. I asked him what they used it for in Germany nowadays." "That was very foolish of you, David," said Professor Leitch mildly, and I noticed that David turned a fiery red. He had a great respect for the little man.

From Scotland, the conversation turned to Ireland, where David Grant had been sent a month before to give a course of lectures at Dublin University. "There's trouble brewing there, all right," he said. "They were fine and pleased when they saw their Saxon oppressor put under the yoke, and heard that the Northern counties were to be restored to them, but they are piping a different tune now that the republic has been put down and there's a German governor in its place." There were still no open signs of trouble, he told us, but the Germans, with a sublime failure to realize the Irish character, were adopting the very methods of control which we had used so disastrously in the past. "What's the good of shooting a dozen Irishmen?" he asked. "You've only created a dozen martyrs in the sacred cause of Irish freedom, and you've inspired a hundred others with the ambition to be shot in similar glorious circumstances. What is more," he added, "I did hear that a long-legged, red-headed fellow called Rosse was on the run in the hills of Connemara. I wonder, would that be the fellow who we used to hear of in the Greyshirts?"

I wondered too. The miserable fate of most of the Greyshirt old guard had been published during the Terror. They were shot out of hand as responsible for civil disturbance. But Rosse's name had disappeared abruptly from the news as soon as he had refused the command of the reorganized Grey Army. Till then I had supposed he had perished in obscurity.

Gradually the conversation languished. Professor Leitch

had fallen silent again, and a mood of depression came over me as I contrasted the stubbornness of the Scots and the fiery resentment of the Irish with what seemed to me the spiritless resignation of the English. The professor seemed to divine my thoughts. He looked at me again with that strangely direct gaze of his, and said:

"We are in the shadows, Mr. Fenton, and they will get darker yet. You are a spectator of our plight, and, as a New Zealander, a member of a young and vigorous people, it may be that you judge this old country a little hardly. Soon, and sooner perhaps than you think, you will go back to your own place, and the best thing you can then do is to tell your countrymen how this horror came about. But tell them too that honesty and justice and truth die hard, and that there may yet be a dawn in our darkness. David and I are among the watchers for that dawn."

Those were the words that inspired this book. We are still waiting for the dawn he spoke of, but I went to my bed that evening strangely comforted.

Chapter Ten

OUTWARD BOUND

HITLER'S star shot onwards and upwards. He was supreme in Europe—France, Scandinavia, the Low Countries, the Balkans, his former partner, Italy, were all his vassals. Without firing a shot he drove the Russians out of their part of Poland and turned Constantinople into a "free German city". India had dissolved into anarchy, and he thought of dispatching a force thither to establish a German *Raj*; in any case, the path to the East was open to him when he chose to take it. The logic of events was hurrying him on to the biggest conquest of all, upon which the others depended. Speed and audacity were still his watchword, and it was unsafe to lose momentum. Across the Atlantic lay the New World, *Unser Amerika*, the finest *Lebensraum* of all.

The day after Hitler had entered London it had been learnt with little surprise that the United States Fleet was holding manoeuvres along the Atlantic seaboard. There is little need to recapitulate for my readers the dramatic and urgent diplomacy of the following few days. It is enough to record that by the end of the week, not only Canada but Australia and our own New Zealand, at the invitation of the Government of the United States, had freely consented to become "temporary American Protectorates". South Africa was, of course, another matter. The long arm of American protection could not be extended so far, and the German subjugation of Britain was hailed with delight by the Nationalist Government of that new republic. Their triumph was short-lived. The German Colonial Army, so long prepared for its task, had arrived at the Cape with lightning speed. The destruction of the pitifully small naval force left in those waters by the defunct Evans Government was accomplished without much difficulty, and is still celebrated by Germany under the resounding title of the "Battle for the South Atlantic". There was no organized land force left to oppose the German landing, and within a very few days the independent South African Republic had been replaced by a German Governor and an administration which differed only from the new régime in Britain in the fact that it was largely composed of Germans from Tanganyika. An abortive native rising was crushed with bloodshed which horrified even the troops who inflicted it.

So now it was the Far East and the Far West which had coalesced to prevent Nazidom from sweeping round the world. With pathetic satisfaction we in London kept reminding ourselves that the great British base at Singapore remained intact, its strength augmented, indeed, by large reinforcements from that Indian Army whose European personnel had no title to remain when the Paramount Power they represented had been brought low. British Malaya presented the strange spectacle of a British possession functioning without a possessor. The unimpaired integrity of this great military and naval bastion in the Far East had a valuable effect in influencing the policy of Japan, and the American Government lent it all possible support for this very reason. The war in China went on, but without affecting the Japanese determination to stop at nothing to exclude the German power from the Pacific. But the key to all was the New World, and particularly that great sentimental, mercantile, Puritan, childlike Power that looked with increasing alarm at Europe from the Capitol and the White House.

It soon became clear that all the resources of Great Britain and her colonies were to be wrung for the last and most ghastly struggle. Standards of living were to be forced down to the limits of human endurance. France was to be dragged in, Italy also; the ships of four navies were to be used to set the foot of Colossus across the ocean.

Only gradually did the British people, in the midst of their suffering, come to realize the stupendous irony of this situation. It had been peace with dishonour, followed by every ounce of the misery which dishonour deserved. Now it was to be war again, and the worst war of all—a war which could only be fought to the bitter end, even if civilization was indeed destroyed in the process. And into that war Great Britain was to be flung helplessly—on the wrong side.

The voice of Hitler thundered from a mighty tribune on the Crystal Palace site. He began calmly, laying just claim to the efficiency with which Britain had been turned into a disciplined and totalitarian State. What he said about the reorganization of industry and finance on the basis of one great Reich stretching from the Vistula to the Atlantic was impressive enough, for he was careful not to express it in terms of human suffering. He did not speak vindictively; he seemed to accept Britannia in that Nordic Family of Nations. Then he had a scornful word for the Jews, and said he knew where they had gone. They had gone to spread their poison in that unhappy country to which all the scum of the democracies had drifted, the United States of America. But in America there were millions of good Germans too, who had preserved themselves from pollution, and were awaiting the day when the blessings of National Socialism would be theirs also, and the Old World would redress the balance of the New. The world could not afford the strange duality which it exhibited to-day—strength, discipline, comradeship on one side of the Atlantic; weakness, confusion, enmity on the other. Frankly, the situation was intolerable. He, the Führer, bore on his shoulders the crushing responsibility for the happiness and security of the peoples of Europe. Should his work be brought to nothing through the schemes of little cliques of politicians who had fraudulently climbed to power in Washington, Rio de Janeiro, and Buenos Aires?

"I have just this to say to you, Mr. so-called President of the United States. Set your house in order, learn the lesson of Europe, cease the harrowing of five million Germans the latchets of whose shoes you are unworthy to unloose. I ask you to tell me—where is Schuschnigg, where is Benesh, where is Beck, where is Churchill? If you dare to oppose yourself to me—me!—their fate will be yours."

I was sitting next to the same American who had spoken

so airily of that long-ago Treaty of St. James's. "Packing off home?" I asked. "You bet," he said, "and you will if you are wise."

Next day, it will be remembered, Japan began staff talks with the countries of the Pan-American Union. A cable from my paper invited me to return home the moment I thought it wise; but I knew that the Nazis were not ready for war immediately, and I did not wish to forsake prematurely my unhappy English friends. In my own mind, I gave myself another month in England.

It was late October, and an Indian summer reigned. At least Elizabeth and I must pay another visit to Ashdene Cottage before we left; and we resolved to take train for Debenford that very week-end. I say we resolved to do so, but to put our resolution into effect was another matter. By that time, travel about England, except on recognized business, was forbidden without a special pass, only to be obtained by submitting to a long cross-examination by a Nazi official and smuggling under the table a substantial bribe. When we reached the Bureau of Communications we found it full of Americans who had come over to Europe on a conducted tour arranged by the Nazis, and now wished to return on the first boat. Elizabeth wondered how many of them had read *It Can't Happen Here* by Sinclair Lewis.

We got our passes at last. The official made many difficulties when he discovered who I was, but I slipped him a ten-mark note. The journey, which we made next day, was slow and uncomfortable, for the resources of the railways were by then almost entirely devoted to military purposes. An S.S. man patrolled the corridor, his sinister silhouette moving regularly across the panorama of the Essex countryside.

Debenford seemed surprisingly unchanged; it was like any other autumn there, and our friends were glad to confirm the impression. "We have a great achievement to report," said Gerald, with a kind of strained cheerfulness. "We have learnt the art of living our own lives. We have forgotten all about politics."

In the white drawing-room, at tea, the scene was magically refreshing. Outside, the reddening trees, the Michaelmas daisies, the great low October sun; within, old friendliness and an English domestic dignity inherited from two centuries ago. The firelight gleamed on the cabinet of Yarmouth pottery and the silken bell-pull; on a small and exquisite Crome; on a whole interior so just and right that one felt at once that it was bound to survive even the struggle of the Titans across the wide Atlantic.

"Of course you have forgotten politics," I said. "What meaning have they here?"

Gerald and Celia Cooke were lucky people. Their income, modest but adequate, came from land, and, as the Nazis were a long way yet from putting into the effect the smallholding policy they had so loudly proclaimed, I imagined that they were as secure economically as one could well be in those days. It really did seem that history had passed them by, or was preserving them to take their due places in the old, lost world which one day, incredibly, would be pieced together again.

We chattered cheerfully, in this beautiful vacuum, and we never mentioned Hitler. Then Elizabeth said that we poor harassed ones wanted to know all about country life.

"Well, of course," said Celia, "we live very quietly now. There is to be no hunting this year—we couldn't afford it in any case; and, well, there isn't really much company, everybody seems to have gone."

She paused, and a look of sadness came over her face. We guessed what tragedies were summed up in those words, "Everybody seems to have gone." But she added: "We should hate to go. Who would wish to leave Debenford, anyway?"

"Who, indeed?" I said. "And it doesn't seem to have altered at all. Especially your garden. What a treasure Ellis is!"

"Oh, didn't you know?" put in Gerald. "We do all our own gardening now. It's—it's rather fun."

There was an awkward pause.

"Ellis was with you a long time," murmured Elizabeth.

"With the family, forty years," said Gerald. "It is very sad."

"Well, these are hard times for all of us," I said, tritely.

"Yes, but we didn't sack him. He's gone away. I think he's at Godalming."

"Godalming? Not——"

"Yes. Godalming concentration camp, where Winston Churchill is. It's dreadful. He was very foolish. He used to talk too much down at the 'Rose Revived'. I warned him over and over again. Of course, he was no danger to the Nazis or anyone else. He was just a nuisance. But when our Small Paddock was commandeered for a rifle range he made some solemn protest, such as spitting at a picture of Hitler. Then they decided he needed a little 'political education', and took him away."

"But couldn't you stop them? Couldn't you explain that

he was a silly old fool, and that you would make yourself responsible for him, or something?"

"Well, I made representations, of course. I went to Ipswich, But you know what it is. People like us don't have much influence nowadays."

"True. And have you heard from Ellis since?"

"No. That was six weeks ago and we have heard nothing. He was seventy-three, poor old chap. I often wonder . . . Of course I pay a kind of pension to his widow—to Mrs. Ellis."

The firelight danced on—in the beautiful vacuum.

"How are those two dear old ladies in the Council cottages whom you were visiting when we were here last?" asked Elizabeth. "Have they recovered from their arthritis, or whatever it was?"

"Yes, I hear they're nearly well again," said Celia, "but of course we don't visit them now."

"You don't visit them?"

"Why, no. Our local Commissioner is most strict on the point. No sick visiting except by the incumbent of the parish and the Authorized Sick Visitor. The Authorized Sick Visitor is Mrs. Bradshaw, whose bedside manner is atrocious. But who knows what Vile stratagem an unofficial person like me might not be hatching in the bedroom of two dear old ladies in a Council cottage?"

Celia laughed mirthlessly at this comic restriction,

A moment later I said to Gerald:

"What about that project of yours for removing the whitewash in the church and looking for wall-paintings? Have you started yet?"

"No," he said.

"You don't mean to tell me that the Germans have forbidden that too?"

"Oh, no. They've raised no objection. But I haven't done anything about it."

Then the dressing bell rang.

It was not, as you may gather, a very successful week-end. Captain von Krausnitz, from the camp on Sutton Walks, came to dinner that night, more or less uninvited, and he had somehow lost his early tact. Little by little the desolation that had descended upon this remote and innocent village was revealed to us. A closer investigation showed that the sullen passivity of a hard-exploited peasant community had settled behind its trim hedges and rose-arbours. The marketing restrictions had hit the place very hard. The farmers were bankrupt and the labourers could hardly live on their wage.

Tyranny had stalked through the lanes like Death, striking where he would—here a village Hampden, like Ellis, sent to the tortures of Godalming or Haworth, there a group of day-labourers, given fifteen minutes to pack their belongings and kiss their wives and children before leaving to help with the harvest in Poland, elsewhere a pretty girl, seduced, without redress, by a drunken S.S. man.

Gerald Cooke had once been public-spirited. He had once been very sensitive to others' suffering. He had served on a dozen local committees, and had flown into a rage if the rent of an old woman's cottage had needlessly been raised by threepence a week. Now he could speak casually of the worst cruelties, and pretend not to be interested in the politics which excluded him from any influence in his village and turned it into a vale of tears. But those who have lived in England since the Captivity will understand.

Ashdene Cottage was really no ivory tower. It could not be, because it contained young Derek, the Cookes' six-year-old son, whose childish enthusiasms were painfully at variance with the atmosphere of calm resignation so carefully built up round him. "Don't ask me what will become of him," said Gerald at a moment when his closest thoughts revealed themselves. "I suppose he will go to no known school, and learn to speak German better than English, and join those horrible Young Englanders. We're all in the same boat, I know, but what a boat!"

On the late afternoon of Sunday, with nearly the whole village, we attended evensong in the lovely old parish church. Here, where the setting sun shone on the backs of the little company and on mouldering poppy-heads through glorious patches of medieval glass, I was aware of the same feeling I had had behind the frosted panes of North Street chapel. The water of life flowed here too.

The familiar Prayer Book office, in a language said to be doomed, had a special poignancy as a precious inheritance from the past, still untouched. Hallowmas was approaching, and the old Vicar spoke of the trials and victories of the saints, who found the means of serving God in every age. Theirs was the only lasting happiness, and it was independent of worldly circumstances.

> *So be it, Lord; Thy Throne shall never,*
> *Like earth's proud empires, pass away.*

The hymn lingered on the ear in the twilit churchyard, and across the village green where a train of lorries marked with the Swastika stood with throbbing engines and the rooks shrieked their raucous good nights.

Next morning on the little station platform, in the five minutes before our train arrived, Gerald unburdened his heart. "Look, Charles," he said hurriedly, walking me up and down the platform, "I've been meaning to ask you this all the time. I'm doing no good here, neither is Celia. We're anomalies, back numbers, relics of another age. Now, can't you get us permission to enter New Zealand? I mean, I could sell out, and smuggle enough of the money out to pass your subsistence tests. Then I could take any kind of job, I don't mind what. I know a good deal about sheep, for instance. Or, if it comes to war, I could join your army, as a private if necessary, and be fighting on the right side.

"It's Derek that we're mainly thinking about," he went on. "I haven't the least idea whether the minor country gentry have any place in the Nazi scheme of things, but, even if they have, could their life be worth living for one moment? It's just hell, I tell you, as it is, though we're pretty much as well off as we were before, and don't lack for a thing. If Celia and I can't get out, honestly I'd gladly stow Derek away on a boat, hoping that he'd be sent to an orphanage or something on the other side."

I hastened to say that I would do everything I could. The train was coming in. I told him that if he could bribe the Nazis at this end I thought I could arrange things at the other. But he would find it difficult to get any professional job or start in business.

"Sheep-farming for me," he called out, as the train got up steam. "Four bob a day"—and a smile of radiant hope lit up his haggard face.

Thus, for the last time, we left our favourite Debenford, unchanged to outward appearance, but in fact just one more Nazi hell. We waved good-bye to our friends, well-to-do, unpersecuted people who yet longed to work as labourers on the other side of the world; and we turned away from the too-beautiful view of the pinnacled tower, the trees, and the sun-glancing estuary.

In London, when we got back, the talk was all about the coming war. It was a relief to discuss someone else's troubles, and this war was in the beginning thought of as a thing that concerned Great Britain no more than indirectly. Then came an announcement which altered things. To some it seemed the last refinement of cruelty, but it strangely quickened the heartbeats of others. There was to be a remobilization of the 25's, 26's, 27's (veterans now), who would form an Army Service Corps and other auxiliaries. They would not be armed—but they would wear their old khaki uniforms, without badges.

Elizabeth felt at once, as I did, strangely exalted and yet sorrowful. The Germans had forgotten something. True, what we thought of could lead nowhere. And yet—was it not something to be thankful for that at least some of our young men could now find an honourable way out?

One did not dare to put one's thoughts into words, but it was not difficult to imagine these comrades in arms brought together again, in the old forage caps and slacks, remembering old times, finding tongue at last for all their pent-up hate and indignation, imagining once again the King's marks upon their worn uniforms—and then rising to perform at last one desperate but gallant deed, which would not be lost to history. Could it be Hitler's one concession, supremely appropriate, to his unhappy victims?

No, there were many explanations, but few supporters of that one. Some said that the Germans had no wish but to humiliate, others that they intended to use the unarmed British as a screen against the enemy, others again that they thought it good propaganda. All thought they were making a mistake.

Smithers came up to me in the office. He was very nearly grinning. "I have been called up again, sir," he said. "Report to-morrow. Would you believe it!"

It was a shock. I had forgotten his age. When he had cleared up certain matters I told him he had better go and spend the rest of the day at Tanner's End with his family. I walked down the narrow stairs with him, and we stood just back from the Fleet Street pavement. He remarked that it would be fine to be in uniform again, just as though he were going to fight for his own country, or were not a peace-loving Nonconformist. "Perhaps we shan't meet again," I said. He looked at me; there was a queer excitement in his eyes. I reminded him that I might have to leave England at any time now, and added: "Goodness knows when the old *Courier* will open its London office again." In the end he decided to break a rule, and drink a toast to our divided fortunes. We crossed over to the "Cheshire Cheese", where it all seemed completely unreal. I told him that if I left I would hand over to his wife any balance there might be in the office account. We talked for the moment to the parrot, and then we went away, and Smithers caught a Number 13 bus, and waved good-bye from the top.

That evening, at Tilbury, as the result of a sudden decision,

I put Elizabeth and our child Julia into a liner bound for New Zealand. Left alone, I became even more conscious of the strangeness of things. The hired car taking me back to Hampstead sped along grey streets of the familiar London pattern, yet it was London no longer, but some weird city on the edge of the world. It was almost a surprise to find the flat still there, a cheerful fire blazing in the grate, and cold supper laid out by the thoughtful Mrs. Jenkins. Everything was in place, including Julia's toys in the nursery; the world had been shaken to its foundations, but still the old golliwog sat up with one eye larger than the other. All the same, Julia and her mother had gone. I looked at my watch, and guessed that the S.S. *Lavinia* was now about opposite Southend pier. What on earth was I doing here, in this city of the dead, waiting helplessly for the start of the worst war of all? I recalled that the next New Zealand boat was due to sail in three weeks' time. Then suddenly I remembered Smithers, and all the other young men who would soon be walking about in khaki forage caps again. There was, after all, something I wanted to stay in London to see.

I began to ask myself questions about a war which everyone regarded as inevitable, but which no-one attempted to describe in advance. How would it begin? What would be Hitler's pretext? Would there be a gigantic naval battle in mid-Atlantic? The whole thing seemed so improbable, part of no natural development. Yet that it was coming I had no doubt. It was a necessity of the Nazi mind.

The next few days were full of rumours of fleet movements. The *Queen Mary* and the *Normandie* were said to be loading troops and supplies at Hamburg. The little band of potential "enemy" journalists in London was breaking up; but a polite Dr. Schultz, insisting, of course, that it was still hoped that war would be averted, assured me that no obstacles would be placed in the way of my departure should the worse come to the worst. I believe the Germans were anxious to let the outside world see to the end how ruthlessly they could bend the British nation to their purpose.

The nameless men in khaki began to appear on the streets. I was told they were forced out of barracks in their leisure hours in order that they might minister to Nazi *Schadenfreude*. Policemen hustled them, Stormtroopers insulted them; but there was still a look of inward excitement on their faces.

Not long afterwards, on a misty morning, I was crossing the Horse Guards Parade when I happened to remember that it was the 11th November, Armistice Day. Glancing at my watch, I saw that the time was ten minutes to eleven. The fancy took me to walk through the arch into Whitehall, and observe a private Two Minutes' Silence in the neighbourhood of the tragic monument which now represented a sacrifice that was doubly vain. To-day we had neither peace with honour nor even peace, and one wondered if it might not have been better if we had made our surrender far back in 1914.

Others besides myself had drifted along to the Cenotaph on that Armistice Day. There was quite a little crowd of women in black, and elderly, shabby men, and a sprinkling of the youths in khaki. As eleven o'clock approached the numbers of the last surprisingly increased; they came up in twos and threes, and soon there must have been a couple of hundred of them. I thought I caught sight of Smithers.

Public assemblages of any kind had long been forbidden, and I expected the police at any moment to come up and disperse the crowd. But the only police in sight were British, engaged on their humble traffic duties, and they appeared to notice nothing exceptional. The normal traffic of the street went on, and some German officials on their way to Downing Street stopped in some surprise to see what was afoot.

Then eleven o'clock struck. The men in khaki, with one accord, sprang to the salute. The elderly men took off their hats, and the Germans, ever responsive to mass discipline and thinking this must be some authorized ceremonial, took their hats off too. The wheeled traffic stopped. Once again there was Silence at the Cenotaph.

It came like manna from Heaven, miraculously. It seemed not to be of human devising. It was the benison of God.

A window snapped open in the Home Office. A shocked, bespectacled, Teuton face looked down and withdrew. Some angry telephoning could be heard inside. Then the Silence came back.

At last—it must have been more than two minutes!—there was a slight stir in the crowd. A khaki-clad figure stepped forward, a rough-looking fellow indeed, but charged at this moment with a kingly, a representative dignity. He laid at the foot of the Empty Tomb a tawdry, untidy object made of scraps of red paper, but which in the eye of the beholders was the most glorious poppy wreath ever made.

That was the end of the Silence. The bespectacled Teuton rushed back to his window, screaming with anger. He was followed by an S.S. man who raised a rifle, took steady aim, and killed the solitary man who was standing before the Cenotaph. At that moment a posse of German foot police emerged from Scotland Yard, and bodies of armed and mounted Black Guards closed in from each end of the street. The civilians ran to take cover in doorways, but the two hundred men in what was once the King's uniform did not run. They formed up in the middle of the road in two parties, and, crying "Long live Britain!" charged at the Germans. They had only their fists; the others had rubber truncheons, horses, pistols. Yet for a moment there was confusion, and then the Germans recovered their balance and began to use their guns.

I saw there was blood on the Cenotaph. I heard one shout of "Mallory! Mallory!" I saw the ex-soldiers falling one by one. A white-haired civilian beside me cried "Come on!" and, wielding his umbrella, rushed into the mellay. I followed him, not really knowing why; he fell before he had run five yards. At the same moment I felt a sharp pain in my left wrist, and immediately afterwards received a blow on the head which knocked me out.

I recovered consciousness in Westminster Hospital. The concussion was not serious, nor was the bullet wound in my wrist, but I was sore all over, and I must have been kicked pretty hard. The nurse told me I was lucky. I had been taken to the Tower with the rest of the wounded, but my Foreign Correspondent's card had been found on me, and that had been enough to send me to hospital. Now I must think no more about it, and rest.

It must have been next day that Dr. Schultz called. "No inquiries," he said, reassuringly, "no cross-questions. I make but a suggestion. The lady matron tells me you will be out of hospital in three days. Your own country perhaps needs you the more? There will be a ship to pull anchor on Friday." He handed me my exit visa, and bounced out, taking my Press pass with him. I turned and went to sleep.

There is little more to tell. I sailed after all, most unheroically, in the S.S. *Anzac* on her next voyage from Tilbury. There were few affairs to settle. My office and flat had both been ransacked, but I had consistently destroyed all significant correspondence. There was no chance of taking out of the country more than one cabin trunk of personal effects, so I arranged for a sale of furniture for the benefit of Mrs. Jenkins. Being shadowed by spies, I avoided all my friends and acquaintances, but I managed to communicate indirectly with the Cookes, giving them the name of a certain official who might, for ten thousand marks or so, get them stowed away in a New Zealand cargo boat before it was too late.

The palm lounge of the *Anzac* belonged to the dear dead days of the P. & O. There were few passengers, because it had now become virtually impossible to leave England by ordinary means. All was incredibly spick and span—a little detached piece of a vanished world floating out, who knew whither? The steward who brought me whisky and soda was surely a character from *Outward Bound*.

Shoeburyness slipped past, and the morning grew cloudy. I noticed a large oil painting, which—no doubt as a tribute from the new Australian owners to the comrades in arms of the original Anzacs—gave a vivid portrayal of the Lancashire Landing. I thought about that desperate enterprise, and many since, and what after all they had led to. I thought of Stephen Mallory, and of the sons of Gallipoli heroes shouting defiance in Oldham market-place; I thought of the Affair of the Cenotaph, in which, the communique had said coldly, "216 mutinous members of the British Army Service Corps and eleven civilians unfortunately lost their lives". These were all failures, with a quality of gallant absurdity; and England was now in chains.

Then I recalled an epitaph which someone, I forget who, had written for the men who had died in that Gallipoli campaign. It went, as far as I could remember, like this:

> *We failed. If, when another sacrifice is needed,*
> *You fail as gloriously, we shall have succeeded.*

I rejoiced to think that ahead lay New Zealand and the war and that the country we were leaving behind was still capable of glorious failures, here and there.

The S.S. *Anzac* entered the Narrows Seas, between the white cliffs and the dunes. Then England disappeared, and I knew that the only way back to her was the long, stern way round by the New World.

EPILOGUE

I WROTE what I thought were the last words of this book a fortnight ago, and went out into the garden of my father's house sick and heavy with the tragedy I had tried to record. I looked across the valley at the steadfast slopes of New Zealand's Southern Alps, and tried to calm my weary and

bewildered brain with the thought of the eternal in nature—
the slow life of the rocks and of the earth and the deep
silence in which it is lived. In a month I would be leaving
with the New Zealand Division for America, and would
plunge once more into the travails of humanity. But for that
month, I said, I would breathe the mountain air and forget
all that lay beyond the hills.

Now, after only two weeks, I have had a reminder, and
yet it is not one which I resent, for it has reminded me of
something not less eternal than the universe—the uncon-
querable soul of man. It is a letter forwarded to me from the
office of my newspaper. The envelope addressed to me at
the *Wellington Courier* itself bore a Wellington postmark
and had been posted within the week. But the letter itself
has only one line of address at the top, "De Profundis", and
it is dated three months back—two months, that is, after my
departure from England. There is no signature, but the
personality of the writer is as clear to me as if I heard his
low, musical voice, and felt again the keen glance of his
blue eyes. I cannot do better than conclude my book by
quoting it:

"Dear Mr. Fenton,
"You will remember the night when three honest men sat
about the fire and took pleasure in a conversation without
fear. I bade you then tell your countrymen of the fate that
had befallen their motherland, and, if I read you then aright,
by now you will be doing so. But I told you then that your
message should not be without hope, and I have since thought
that I should have given you more ground for such hope than
I did at the time. I accepted my young friend's guarantee of
your honesty, and indeed liked and trusted you myself, but
too much depended on my silence for me to be entirely open
with you. Even now I shall not be able to tell you a great
deal, for I, and many others with me, stand as guardians over
a life which was born in silence and suffering and which
must be nursed in secrecy and watchfulness. It is the infant
life of freedom that we guard—a freedom not only of the
body but of the spirit—and, if this child can be reared un-
harmed to man's estate, it may be that a Britain shall arise
again, greater and nobler for the sufferings she had endured.
Remember, Mr. Fenton, that our former freedom died long
before the German tyrant set his foot on our necks. It grew
sick when we put the safety of ourselves before the freedom
of others, and, though there was a time when it looked as
though it might recover, its life was finally extinguished

when we made peace with the powers of darkness.

"I have said that I cannot tell you many secrets. What I will tell you is of things done and endured—things that our oppressors have kept hidden from the world—and you reading them may learn something of what is being prepared. Every day men meet in desert places—in darkened rooms, in forests, and in lonely valleys—and the gospel of freedom is passed from mouth to mouth and the light of hope dawns again on forlorn faces. These are some of the stories that are told:

"There was an engine-driver, called Angus Maclean. He learnt one night at Euston that he was to drive a train-load of German troops—the 29th Regiment—to Scotland. Before the train pulled out of London he had communicated his knowledge to a friend, and it was straightway known in Scotland at what hour Angus Maclean would drive his train across the Forth Bridge. All through the night Angus Maclean drove his train northwards, and his only fear was that he should fail to reach the bridge at the appointed hour. He was not late. As his train began to roll across the bridge there was as explosion which shattered the central span, and Angus Maclean and his engine, and the trainload of troops behind it, were plunged into the Forth.

"There was an aeronautical engineer, called Philip Parsons. The Germans demanded that he should help them to build their warplanes. At first he refused to work, but his wife and young child were taken from him as hostages for his obedience, and he was forced to consent. Then a workmate told the Germans that before they had taken over the rule of the country Parsons had discovered a secret that would make it possible to produce faster aeroplanes than the world had yet seen. His German masters summoned him, and told him that if the secret was not in their hands by the next morning his son would be shot and his wife sent to the troops in Poland. Philip Parsons went out and told a friend what had befallen him. The friend gave him a promise, and the next morning Parsons went to his masters as he had been bidden. But instead of his secret plans he produced a pistol and shot three of those in authority dead before he took his own life. And while those shots were fired certain men came to the place where his wife and child were confined and delivered them, and the Germans have not seen them again. But they are alive and well cared for, for this was the promise that Parsons had received from his friend, and his young son shall grow to be a credit to his father.

"There was an office-cleaner called Mrs. Ambleside. She

was poor and elderly, and, after they had got tired of making the Jews do it, she was employed by the Germans to wash the floors and sweep the dust at Bush House. When she came there she knew no German, and she had only the dimmest idea of the vast organization which had its headquarters there. But the Germans had not troubled to discover that Louisa Ambleside had had a nephew who had been beaten to death as a Socialist in Stoke Poges camp. Even if they had known I doubt if they would have been disturbed, for she was a tired-looking, elderly woman, and there were many who had greater cause for grievance. But Mrs. Ambleside had the imagination to see that she might some day use her employment as a means towards vengeance for her nephew, so she learnt German. This is a duty enjoined upon all of us, but the workers have neither the time nor the energy for it, and on the whole their ignorance is overlooked provided that they send their children to the official schools of instruction. But Mrs. Ambleside learnt German at the age of fifty-three, and learnt it so well that she could understand what her employers were talking about. No doubt she had a neglected capacity for languages, for she learnt it in an extraordinarily short time. Meanwhile she kept her eyes and ears open at Bush House, and discovered a good deal about the work which was going on there.

"In due course Mrs. Ambleside met one of those who work with me, for we have learnt not to neglect the humble and obscure. To him she told what she had discovered, and, when she understood the cause for which he was working, she offered him her services. They were accepted, and Mrs. Ambleside became one of our outposts. A few weeks ago she found at Bush House the secret file containing a list of the informers stationed in the towns and villages up and down the country. It was a bulky document, but every night she succeeded in abstracting a page or two, and brought it home where there was one ready to copy it. Every morning she restored the copied page so that it should not be missed. When there were only three pages left uncopied she was caught tampering with the file. She died after only two days of interrogation, for mercifully she had a weak heart. But the inquisitors never learnt from her that she understood German; they never learnt for whom she had been working; and they still do not know how much of their secret is in our hands.

"I could tell you many of these stories, and indeed one of my purposes in writing was to ensure that these names should not be forgotten. But I am reminded that the document must not be too bulky, and indeed there are too many names to be recorded. I could tell you of working men, mechanics and unskilled labourers, who have run the risk of death and torture in order to hamper the running of just that tiny section of the German machine in which they are involved. I could tell you of others who live a hunted life, of those who have died or are ready to die to keep the secret of their comrades. Among them indeed is that long-legged, red-headed rebel of an Irishman who once led a great number of his fellow Greyshirts towards destruction. Now, in contrition, he has taken for himself the name of another red-head, Judas, and yet he wears his penance with an air, and the name is one to conjure with in the waste places of his native land, where arms are hidden beneath the peat stack. What is more, he has made the cause of his fiery-hearted countrymen one with that which inspires the quiet English and the stubborn Scots. There is more unity in these islands to-day than there has ever been before in all their history. It is the task of my fellowship to make that unity a positive and constructive force, and not just a negative reaction to oppression.

"It is not so difficult a task as you might think. A great soberness and patience has been born out of our subjection, and yet the spirit of the people is not dead. For a while it slept, stunned into resignation, but all the time it was being kept alive, not by the intellectuals or the thinkers, still less by the politicians and talkers, but by the greatest and most inarticulate section of the population, the working-class. For the workers were acquainted with suffering, and to them hardship was nothing new. The young men might be led away after this catchword or that, but as they married and had children and laboured to support those children they learnt deeper truths. Now the fellowship of the poor has been extended to embrace all classes in Britain, and we are all learning the same lessons together. We have learnt to refrain from rhetoric and to mistrust meaningless catchwords, for it was by such means that this country was enticed towards anarchy and ruin. Now our captors have taught us the value of silence, unless there is a true thing to be said and a true man to hear it spoken. We have learnt, too, by bitter experience, that romantic gestures and demonstrations are of no avail against the strength of tyranny. The Armistice Day massacre, of which I am told you were a witness, was one such lesson. We have learnt that, in the cause for which we are fighting, every word must be weighed, and every action judged by the fruit which it is likely to bear. We have learnt to husband our strength and to control our energy, and yet when the right moment comes to expend it all without stint in the service of the cause.

"Yet all this knowledge, hard-won and precious though it is, is only contributory to the two great principles which our poverty and subjection have taught us. The first is the need for freedom—an equal freedom for every man and every people upon the earth. The second is that the road to such freedom lies only in the denial of self and the sacrifice of personal ends. It is only by sacrifice and the brotherhood of sacrifice that the people of Britain will grow strong enough to regain their freedom, and it is only by still further sacrifice that freedom shall put an end to all further chance of tyranny upon the earth.

"Before the war, we in this country had the foundation of such freedom in the laws and constitution under which we lived. The very cause for which we went to war was a belated recognition of the principles of freedom. The world, too, had the foundation of brotherhood in the League of Nations. But national self-seeking destroyed the brotherhood of the League, and private greed and selfish fear at last put an end to freedom in Great Britain. It has taken all this suffering and slaughter to teach us the value of what we threw away.

"Already our new-found strength is beginning to tell. Our oppressors look at us strangely, angry and fearful at something they do not understand. They are like the Egyptians walking in darkness, of whom the Wise Man wrote: 'For the whole world shined with clear light and none were hindered in their labour: over them only was spread a heavy night, an image of the darkness which should afterwards receive them: but yet were they unto themselves more grievous than the darkness.' And again: 'For wickedness, condemned by her own witness, is very timorous, and being pressed with conscience, always forecasteth fearful things.'

"This fear has come upon the Germans in Britain and elsewhere, but they do not know what they fear. Sometimes a blind panic comes upon them, and they commit new outrages on the bodies of their victims. Sometimes they even make overtures to us, and seek comfort and justification from those they have wronged. Meanwhile the great machine of conquest and empire which they built runs slower and less smoothly, in spite of all the urgency of an impending conflict. It is as though it was impeded by its own magnitude. There is a feeling that, instead of a weapon for further conquests, it is becoming a trap for its constructors. Even the enforced migrations which they devised to break our spirit have turned against them. For by this means the germ of freedom was spread among the captive peoples, and it is now not one nation or another but a whole continent that waits and watches for the light.

"I greet you, Fenton, as one who may have a hand in the rebuilding of this world when the night is departed. Whether I shall meet you in that new day I do not know, but that it is on its way I cannot doubt. We have watched for the dawn, and already the darkness grows pale."